Song of the Cicada

Laura Holt

Song of the the Cicadas

Also by Laura Holt:

Fathoms Below

Fathoms Above

Fathoms Between

Fathoms Across

Village of Salt and Sorrow

This is a work of fiction. Names, characters, businesses, places, events, and incidents are either the products of the author's imagination or used in a fictitious manner. Any resemblance to actual persons, living or dead, or actual events is purely coincidental.

Table of Contents

For every girl with a broken heart who chose to be angry about it. You had a reason.

"The scariest monsters are the ones that lurk within our souls..."
~ Edgar Allan Poe

1
Lir is Dead

"Lir is dead."

I stand, barefoot, in the one-room cabin on the moor that is my home, unable to reconcile the words coming through the receiver. The name of my best friend, my life, my other half, the man who was supposed to be my husband, the only person I have ever loved and trusted, echoes in my ears like the mournful cry of a gull. Sand from the seashore on the other side of the cliffs, forever blowing in through the cracks in the walls where the stones have separated over time and underneath the doorjamb, is gritty beneath my toes. I was sweeping before the phone rang, the birch broom in my hand now a useless, forgotten thing.

The signs of summer are all around me. The bleating of the sheep in their paddock, demanding to be sheared. The warm sunlight cascading through the open window past the short woolen curtains I'd knitted a few weeks ago to replace the old, moth-eaten ones, dancing across the still hearth like fairies. The billows, which I haven't used since the first spring thaw of the year, hanging next to the stove. The dozen or so glass jars on the counter freshly washed and sparkling and ready for canning. The steady, familiar *chirrup-chirrup* of the cicadas that come to lay their eggs in the old oak tree in the backyard. Only it may as well be winter for how cold I feel.

I am only half-listening as my sister keeps talking on the other end of the line about how the police had searched as long as they could, longer really than they should have, and it had been a hard decision for everyone to decide to finally close the case. How there would still be a memorial, even though Lir's body had never been found, and I would need to come to town with her for a few days, to attend and handle the legal matters. Do I want her to come to get me? Or meet at the train station? I struggle to breathe, to stay alert, but the air doesn't come. My throat feels tight, constricted as if death has wrapped its icy fingers around my neck and begun to squeeze the life from me.

I panic at the thought, tiny, animalistic mewling sounds bursting from my lips. The sound reminds me of the burrow of field mice I had found at the back of the barn last year, the tiny, fearful squeaks the little blind babies had made as they squirmed around in the hay when I touched their downy-soft backs with a careful, wonderous finger.

I had kept the barn shut up for weeks, unable to bring myself to kill them even though I knew they would get into the cupboard if given half a chance, careful not to let anything inside that might eat them until they were old enough to see and run around on their own.

"Clare? Clare, are you there? What's going on? Talk to me. Say something." My sister's voice, tinny and echoing, as if she was driving through a tunnel on the other end of the accursed phone, cuts through the deafening pulse of blood in my ears. It is a hideous green plastic thing, one of the few modern appliances I keep. I barely ever use it, except when Arleen calls to check up on me. Half the time, it doesn't even work. The electricity up here, this close to the cliffs, is as unreliable as the weather. Its cord, I realize, is the thing wrapped around my neck. Somehow, I had gotten tangled in it.

I rip it away and gasp in a huge breath of air that hurts my throat. Except I don't answer my sister, don't tell her that I am still here, that our connection has not been lost, and that I am in no way, shape, form, or fashion okay.

Instead, I scream.

"Clare?"

Rush Kelly, the farmhand who helps me out on the croft, appears in the doorway. He is a big man, with long, awkward limbs and a head like a pumpkin who looks older than his mere thirty years from a lifetime of working outside in all manner of weather. Yet he is one of the few from County Kirk who is not afraid to come near me. His hands are caked in grime from where he's been working in the orchard. When I don't reply, his bushy eyebrows draw together in an expression of fear and concern, and he steps over the threshold.

I can still hear my sister squawking through the speaker yet can no longer make out what she is saying. It doesn't matter, I realize. I hate her. She is my only living family, and even though she abandoned our way of life for a more comfortable one in the city the moment she came of age, I love her with the kind of fierce passion that moves mountains, boils seas, and starts wars. But right now, at this moment, I hate her.

With another furious cry, I hurl the phone across the room. It hits the stone wall and shatters. Nimbus, my orange fluffball and my only companion aside from Rush, leaps down from her perch on the windowsill with a yowl, her afternoon nap disturbed, and streaks through the hired help's legs and out the door.

The sound of her caterwauling breaks something in me. Some last thread holding me together. I fall to my knees, dropping the broom with a clatter.

"Clare!" Abandoning all pretense, Rush crosses to me in two steps and grabs me by the shoulders. "Clare, what is it? Are you unwell?"

I shake my head, furious at him, at my sister, at the

21

phone, at my traitorous heart, at the world. Tears prick my eyes and spill down my cheeks. I won't say it. Perhaps if I don't, if I keep the answers to his questions safely locked away inside my throat, it won't be true. It can't be true! There has to be some mistake. Someone is playing a cruel trick on me, the way the village children used to when we were little, and when I find out who it is, I will make them pay.

Rush shakes me, my head flopping on my shoulders like a rag doll. "What is it?" A hint of panic tinges his voice now.

"Lir is dead!" I shout the words, unable to hold them back any longer, and hurl them at him like a javelin, wanting him to feel at least a small measure of my pain.

It has the desired effect. He recoils, releasing me, mouth dropping open. Yet no sooner has the confession left my lips than a new weight, of helplessness and a horrible, dark acceptance, covers me like a shroud.

"Lir is dead." My voice croaks, catching on to the last syllable.

I clasp my hands, as if about to pray, though what words might leave my lips that any deity would listen to, I do not know. I have never been prone to any religion outside of my craft. I sway from side to side, feeling suddenly drunk, untethered, a boat unmoored without a port. I stare up into Rush's kind, weathered face, beseeching him without words to tell me I am wrong. Not to worry. This is only a dream, and soon I will wake up to find that everything is all right, because it has to be. The alternative—any alternative—is too terrible to contemplate.

Instead, I watch as his blue-gray eyes fill with pity and sorrow.

The sight is too much, like the final sunset on the last day of the world. My heart skitters to a stop and sits

22

like a stone in my chest for a long moment, before starting to beat again. Spots dance at the edges of my vision, threatening unconsciousness. I blink them away, struggling to remain lucid as his arms go around me, pulling me against his chest.

The action rekindles my fury. How dare he try to comfort me when nothing can ever fix this? I fight his grip, tiny fists beating against the front of his thick cotton work shirt with all the force of a sand gnat until the weight of my grief becomes too much to bear. Then, I sag against him, limbs going limp, eyelids fluttering closed, and let the faint take me away to blissful darkness.

2

Not a Big Fan of Pollution

I stand before the full-length mirror on the wall, staring at the white sheet draped over the glass. It's a tradition in honor of the dead, to ensure their souls don't get trapped in the netherworld on the way to the afterlife.

Lir is a soul, floating somewhere in the ether above my head.

It does not seem real, though I covered the mirror myself shortly after he was pronounced dead, the sheet starchy and stiff beneath my fingers from months spent folded in the closet. I averted my eyes as I did, not wanting to face the broken girl looking back.

I can picture her now, as clearly as if I could see her. The red curls, too long and unkempt. The pale, freckled skin. The slight, upturned nose and narrow shoulders, made more pronounced than usual from not eating. The green eyes swollen from crying.

A week has passed since my sister's phone call and Lir's missing person's case officially turned into a cold case. Files and photographs, statements from witnesses, friends, and family, all packed away into a cardboard box and shoved onto a shelf at the back of the two-cell police station, where it would spend the rest of its days gathering dust. It hadn't taken long for the news to spread through the entire village like a wildfire I couldn't put out. Only maybe he's been dead a lot longer than that. Nobody knows.

Nobody knows where Lir is.

Seven years ago, he was on his way back from County Kirk to Galway, where he was attending university. Only he never made it. The school called his parents first when he didn't show up for classes. When they couldn't get in touch with him, and no one they asked could either, they alerted the police. The detective assigned to the case found his automobile abandoned on the side of the road a few kilometers outside of Kirk, the cardboard mug of coffee in the cupholder still warm. He never even made it to the motorway.

After that, Lir's disappearance became an official missing person case. They dusted his car for fingerprints and searched it for signs of foul play, but found nothing disturbed or out of place. No drop of blood, no strand of hair or scrap of cloth on the seats. Not so much as a footprint on the grassy bank. Even the keys were still in the ignition, the engine grumbling and running low on petrol. The only fingerprints they found other than Lir's were his parents, his brothers, and mine. They questioned us all, of course, but we'd all been in the car on numerous occasions, so they quickly let it go.

When the police failed to find him, his parents hired a series of private detectives to work with them. Each one did something different. One interviewed all his friends, family, acquaintances from school, and anyone who might have some idea of where he had gone. Another searched his flat, car, and luggage for clues. A third, a man with a handlebar mustache and portly belly, investigated the service station where he'd stopped for snacks and a caffeinated beverage on the way out of town the day he disappeared. A fourth even used bloodhounds to comb the stand of scraggly oaks that lined the winding road along the sea cliffs where his car was found. But in the end, each one said the same thing.

Lir was gone, and he wasn't coming back.

I guess his parents finally decided to accept that.

Rush raps his knuckles against the doorframe,

25

startling me so badly that I jump. He removes his hat sheepishly, letting his auburn curls tumble free. He is wearing his nicest pair of pants, the ones without the grass stains, and a freshly pressed shirt.

"Sorry, Clare. I just-I wanted to see if you were ready to go."

"Give me a minute."

Legs still trembling from the jolt of unexpected adrenaline, I dismiss him and turn back to the mirror. I watch him duck his head obediently and retreat outside, where he will wait by the cart until I emerge, as I attempt to tame my hair into a bun. When all but several stubborn sprigs are wound against the nape of my neck, I call it good enough and set the wide-toothed wooden comb onto the small dressing table. As I do, my fingers brush against something stuck halfway underneath the hand-carved jewelry box. Forehead furrowing, I pull it out and flip it over.

It is a picture, one of the grainy, polaroid kind my mum was so fond of, of Lir and me from our last year of grade school. We stand on my front stoop in our caps and gowns, laughing at something his mum said while trying to get us to cheese for the photo. I can see Arleen's face peeking out from the background behind us, never wanting to intrude but also needing to not feel left out of what she saw as our more grown-up relationship. He looks so vibrant, so young, so healthy, so alive, his eyes alight with mirth and a smile stretched across his face. The sight hits me like a punch to the gut.

How can someone like that be here one minute, and the next, be gone?

Laying the picture facedown where I'd found it, I walk across the room and step out into the sunshine. Rush is standing next to the cart, exactly like I thought he would be, feeding a handful of hay to Rhiannon, our sorrel-backed mare.

"I'm ready."

He looks up with a jerk of his chin, his turn to be startled this time. His eyes widen at the sight of me in my good dress, my hair pulled back off my shoulders so that the blush of my cheekbones is visible. Not a lot, but enough that I notice. He swallows, throat bobbing, before holding out a hand to help me up onto the bench seat of the wagon.

No cars for us. Fuel is too expensive, and besides, I'm not a huge fan of pollution.

He clambers up beside me, clunky as always, too big no matter where he goes, and gives the reins a gentle slap. Rhiannon begins her slow, easy plod out of the yard, and we rattle down the road toward the village.

I look over at him, one hand attempting to hold my hair in place, and lightly touch his arm. He glances at me, keeping one eye on the road in case we hit a stray rock, a question clear in his gaze. I attempt to smile and it kind of works.

"Thank you. For coming with me, I mean."

"You're welcome."

This time when he gulps, it has nothing to do with the way I look and everything to do with the sorrow we both feel. For a second, I think I also see a flash of regret cross his face. But it's there and gone so quickly, I'm sure I imagined it.

"Lir and I were never as close as the two of you, but I still considered him a friend."

I nod. There is nothing else to say to that, not really. We ride the rest of the way into town in silence.

27

3

A Song about Lost Love

Lir's memorial is at the small church near the village center. The brass bell in the steepled tower rings as we pull up to the sidewalk, the metallic chimes echoing off of the stone buildings. Rush hops down and ties off the horse to a nearby lamppost so she doesn't wander before he helps me out of the cart. I shield my eyes from the sun with my free hand and peer up the stairs at the open doors.

I hate this place. The suffocating press of the walls and pews with too many bodies crammed into not enough space. The judgmental sermons of fire and brimstone and other such horrible fates awaiting a woman who does not obey a man. The inescapable reminder of what those kinds of men did to my ancestors—how they tried to control them and, when that failed, tortured them, burned them, drowned them, hung them, turned them to stone.

But faith was always important to Lir. He believed in the goodness of God, in salvation for all souls, male and female, and things like love, forgiveness, and hope. So, I push aside my revulsion and go inside, Rush following at my heels.

Flowers decorate the sanctuary, stuffed in vases and set on every flat service. Wild shamrock clovers on the altar and cowslip line the aisles, and soft blue sheep's-bit blanket the empty casket where Lir's body ought to lie but doesn't. I can hear their dying cries and feel the last remnants of life leaching out of their severed stems. I have to resist the urge to cover my ears with my hands. To not draw any more attention to me than is necessary.

D'arcy sees me first.

D'arcy is younger than his brother by only three minutes and identical in every way save for their personalities. He steps around the simpering biddy offering him her condolences and walks toward me, purpose in every stride. He has traded his uniform for coat and tails, his hair falling to one side. A pocket watch, gold, with a bright purple thistle carved into the front, dangles from his breast. Heads turn to follow his progress, to see where he is going, and I hear the first of the whispers stir, my name falling from their lips like a curse, a blessing, a spell.

I straighten my back, unwilling to let them chase me off today. Not when I have more of a reason than every one of them put together to be here. I lock eyes with D'arcy, letting him know I see him coming, and that I will wait for him to reach me before I go any farther, and my world seems to turn on its head. My vision shimmers, and it is suddenly Lir walking toward me instead of his brother. I gasp, sweat making my palms damp. Then D'arcy puts his arms around me, drawing me into a tight hug, and the illusion vanishes, a bubble burst too soon.

Trying not to let anyone see how shaken I am, I wrap my arms around his neck and close my eyes. The black of my eyelids is comforting.

"I'm so sorry, D'arcy." My voice sounds choked, even to me.

"Yeah, me too," he answers gruffly, giving my waist a final squeeze before releasing me and holding me at arm's length. His eyes, the same shade of violet-blue as Lir's, study me. "How are you holding up, Clare?"

I shrug noncommittally. "How do you think?"

D'arcy nods in understanding. "Yeah." He turns to Rush as if noticing him standing there in my shadow and shakes his hand. "Thanks for keeping an eye on her way out there. The moor is no place for a lady, especially at a

29

time like this."

"Just doing my duty, sir," Rush says politely, his country brogue coming out stronger when he's nervous. "But if you don't mind my saying, Miss Clare can take care of herself."

"Of course."

I step around D'arcy as he and Rush continue to converse in low voices—about what finally made the police stop looking, what everyone thinks happened to Lir, how D'arcy is dealing with the failure of being the detective who couldn't find his twin—and find his youngest brother Jack in the crowd. He is sitting on the steps of the pulpit beside the casket, his head in his hands. I tap his shoulder to get his attention, and he looks up at me with red-rimmed eyes. I can tell he's been crying and was trying to hide it.

My already broken heart cracks a little bit more.

"Oh, Jack." I kneel in front of him, dress bunching around my knees. Pretense be damned. He holds it for a moment, lips trembling against the floodgates. Then all fifteen "manly" years of him crumples into my arms like the child he'd been when I first met him.

"He's gone, Clare. I kept—I kept thinking he was going to come back. That he was hiding somewhere, you know? Working on that novel he was talking about starting. But-but he's gone." He sobs big, ugly, hiccupping cries that make his shoulders shake, no longer caring who hears or sees him as the grief takes over.

I rub his back as fresh tears run unbidden down my face, pooling, salty and hot, in the corners of my mouth. "I know."

Spent, he sits back, sniffling, and wipes his nose. I give him a last comforting pat then get to my feet and turn to face his parents.

They are holding hands, something I have never

30

seen them do in all the years I've known them. No shows of affection for the Flynns. They both look shell-shocked, as if they still haven't entirely accepted this is happening. Their voices are monotone, their eyes blank and glassy, as they thank each person who passes by the coffin for coming.

When they see me, their expressions change.

Mrs. Flynn grabs me in a choking hug, whispering fiercely in my ear that Lir would have been glad I came. Mr. Flynn takes my small hands in his much bigger ones, their palms warm and smooth. Unlike mine, callused from years of farm work. Once again, Lir's eyes stare down at me from someone else's face.

"He cared about you so much, Clare. Never forget that."

I nod, unable to speak, and look around for Rush. If I stay here another second, with these people who loved Lir as much as I did, I am going to lose it.

Rush is at my side in an instant, as if he heard my thoughts, and takes my arm.

"Come on, Clare. Let's go sit down."

I smile weakly at Lir's dad, pull my hands out of his, and let Rush lead me to the front pew, which was reserved for family and me.

I wasn't blood family, but I was still close enough to count.

He leaves me there, then goes to take an empty seat next to my sister a few rows back. She wears a big hat with a veil that half covers her face, so I almost don't recognize her. But the strand of pearls resting against the neck of her pale gray dress—the ones I plucked from the mouths of oysters and strung together for her as a child—are a dead giveaway.

She sniffs, lifts a handkerchief to blot at her eyes,

and I turn away as the doors to the sanctuary close behind us, signaling the start of the service. Jack and his parents join me in the front row. D'arcy climbs up on stage.

He looks oddly out of place, standing behind the podium where the priest would normally be. Glancing at the waiting crowd, he pulls a stack of notecards out of his pocket, shuffles through them until he finds his place, and clears his throat.

"Thank you all for coming today to celebrate the life of my brother, Lir Flynn. I'm not going to say a lot of lengthy words about the kind of person Lir was. His character spoke for itself to everyone who met him. Nor will I pretend to know much about what comes after death. Lir was the spiritual one of the two of us, but he believed that there was a better place, call it Heaven or Valhalla or whatever, for those people who did honest, good things in their lives." He gives a low chuckle.

"I envied my brother for a lot of things. How easily he made friends. His brain, especially when he made A's without studying and I had to cram for a C. His ability to find love."

He looks at me then, his eyes deep, drowning pools of unshed tears, and I clasp my hands together so tightly my knuckles turn white.

"More than anything, though, I always wished I had his faith. So today, that's what I want to leave with. What I hope we all leave with. Faith, that wherever Lir is, he's in a better place. Thank you." He descends the steps, stuffing the cards back into his pocket, and sits down by his brother.

I take a deep breath, rise to my feet, and mount the stage, the weight of the congregation's eyes bearing down on me. I ignore them as best I can, although every nerve in my body is screaming for me to run, to flee this place and never look back, place my hands atop my heart, and close my eyes.

It's my turn.

The day after Arleen had called me with the news, Mrs. Flynn came by the house, asking me to give the speech honoring Lir's memory. But I refused. There were no words to describe what he had meant to me, what he had meant to everyone who had known him, and how he'd touched countless lives simply by being who he was. When she realized I wouldn't budge, she acquiesced, and said D'arcy could give the speech, if I would at least sing a hymn. It was, she added before I could protest, what Lir would have wanted.

I never was able to say no to him, not even when we were kids. I guess that's one thing that will never change.

The song I sing is an old one, a lullaby in the old tongue about a maiden's lost love. My mother used to sing it to me during stormy weather while she brushed the brambles from my hair. Life is filled with all kinds of storms, she would tell me at the end, both literal and figurative, and if we learn to weather them, we can get through anything.

The sound is mournful, tinged in hope. I cannot think of anything more fitting for today.

When I finish, there is only silence, punctuated here and there by a small sob. Lowering my hands to my sides, I hurry back to my seat as the preacher comes down the aisle and stands beside the empty casket. His pinched mouth and too-tight cheekbones are the only signs that he does not approve of the song I sang or the speech D'arcy gave.

"Brothers and sisters in Christ, it is always tragic when a life is taken from us too soon. Yet even in a time as dark as this, we can find peace in God's promise that Lir Flynn is now in Heaven. One day, rest assured, we will see him again." He holds out his hands. "Let us stand and recite the Lord's Prayer together."

I rise obediently, not wanting to stick out. Yet, I do not recite the words with the rest of those gathered. Instead, I stare at the oakwood box, the symbol of Lir's ended life.

He should have been in there, eyes closed, hands folded peacefully, and dressed in his favorite outfit. Only he wasn't. No one knew where he was, and now, they never would.

It wasn't fair. I wanted to scream like a woman possessed, to rush down the aisle and upend the casket in the hopes that his body would magically tumble out. Then I could grab him and shake him by the shoulders until he opened his eyes and apologized for putting me through this. Only I couldn't, because it wouldn't work. He wasn't there. And even if he had been, it wouldn't have mattered.

Lir would never wake up again.

4
Another Symbolic Saying Goodbye

I stand between Rush and D'arcy at the graveside service after leaving the church. Another symbolic saying goodbye that means nothing. The wind has begun to pick up, drawn by the grief howling inside my chest, and their bodies block most of the chill.

The preacher says another prayer, something about committing Lir's body to the ground and his soul to Heaven, then gives each of us a small handful of dirt. I close my fist around it and feel some get under my fingernails, before tossing it onto the top of the casket.

Two men lower the casket into the grave.

The lid is closed, just like the book of Lir's life.

I clutch Rush's and D'arcy's arms as if they are lifelines anchoring me to land. Without them, I will drift off into an endless sea of grief. When the men begin to shovel fresh earth into the hole, I finally give in to the sobs trying to rip free from my chest.

Lir is gone. And with him, a part of me.

5
What Lir Would Have Wanted

The whole village is waiting at Lir's house for visitation after we return from the private service at the cemetery. Or rather, Lir's family's house now, I guess.

There are tons of food, all brought by the kindly, peach-cheeked ladies from the church: maple ham, baked beans, corn on the cob, and apple cinnamon pie. It reminds me of how Lir and I made ourselves sick one Yule dinner after eating too much.

I don't get anything to eat this time. I am afraid if I do, I will hurl again.

I leave Rush on the couch in the living room, talking to my sister about our new calf that was born a few weeks ago, and go looking for D'arcy instead. He is sitting on the back porch, alone, long legs hanging over the side. A half-eaten plate of roast chicken and potatoes rests on his lap.

I sit down beside him. "Hi."

"Hey." He turns his head to look at me, his inspector's eyes taking in my missing plate. "You're not eating?"

I shake my head. No point in lying to him. He'll see right through it. "I don't think I'll ever eat again."

"Do you think that's what Lir would have wanted?" He raises his eyebrows at me, his voice accusatory.

"Do you?" I counter.

He doesn't have anything to say to that.

6

Never Truly Alone

Nature witches like me have always lived on the moor at the edge of County Kirk, where the land ends and the sea begins at the cliffs of Brigid. With our powers, we control the weather, keep the land healthy and whole, help the crops to grow by providing the right amounts of sun and rain, protect the village from harmful storms, and guide the change of the seasons from one to the next.

Growing up, my mother told me that we were descended from Brigid, the goddess of the dawn and the spring, who rose from her home each morning at the edge of the ocean. It was there that she met Torin, a handsome prince of the Celts, and fell in love. Later, she bore him a daughter, Manan, a mortal like her father, but with all the powers of her celestial mother.

Wanting to be with Torin forever, Brigid begged her father, Eochaid Ollathair, the great god and all-father, to turn him immortal. He granted her wish. Yet too late, she realized that she had forgotten to also ask for him to have eternal youth.

Unable to die, poor Torin continued to age, growing so ancient and withered that he could no longer move, until at last Brigid was unable to bear seeing her lover in such pain. Out of pity, she transformed him into a cicada, thus allowing him to shed his old skin and don a new one each year. Unwilling to live without him, even for a brief time, the goddess transformed herself into a great golden hare so that when Torin retreated into his chrysalis every autumn and winter she could go into hibernation, then emerge with him again in the spring.

It is for this reason that rabbits, above all other creatures, are sacred to the women in our family. Our power is tied to their well-being, their lifeforce, the same way it is to the soul of the rabbit with gold fur and bright blue eyes who pops up at the same time the cicadas do every spring, as ageless as she is divine.

Over the centuries, our family has worn many different mantles and carried many different names since our original ancestor Manan passed her divine abilities down to her daughter, and her daughter after that. We have been queens, abbesses, saints, midwives, and soldiers. My name, Sage, belonged to my father, a railroad worker from Kinsale, who moved here in 1998 to help with the new line being put in that would run from Cork to Dublin.

He met my mother at a Beltane celebration a few weeks later. She was the most beautiful girl in the village, with pink ribbons woven through her ruby tresses, and he was a handsome youth in his own right, full of fancy words and big dreams of making it rich off his trade. It did not take long for him to work up the courage to ask her for a dance, then a kiss. Soon, they realized they had fallen in love.

They were married within a year. After another, they had me, and three years later, my sister followed. But country living is not for the faint of heart, especially on the croft, where the wind is as cold and merciless during the winter as it is loving and gentle during the spring. And the ground requires a firm hand, or a magical one, to yield any fruit.

He left when I was ten.

My mother raised us on her own, my sister and me, taught us everything we needed to know about the land and nature and our powers until a nasty bout of influenza took her from us two weeks before Arleen's sixteenth birthday. I took over where she had left off, tending the croft, seeing to the animals and the plants, selling my services to the people in the village who would buy them, and raising my sister far away from the scorn of the ones who would not.

As soon as she turned eighteen, she left for Galway, drawn by the bright lights, well-paying jobs, and ease of modern living, leaving me behind to tend to our family's legacy alone.

Only thanks to Lir, I was never truly alone.

7

The Stab of Envy

My powers have always been stronger than those of my mother and sister. My mother, while a skilled herbalist, took weeks to sprout a full field of wheat, while I was calling down rainstorms and calming blizzards from my cradle.

My sister, on the other hand, seems content with her hairless cat named Mr. Bunkers whom Nimbus would eat for breakfast and balcony of potted plants in the city, where she starts the day on a yoga mat and finishes it with a glass of wine and the latest reality show on TV.

I watch her now as she bustles around the cabin, making me some tea, cell phone in one hand, and I take in the low-slung jeans and too-tight shirt that she changed into as soon as we got home. A tiny bit of her midriff pokes out below the hem, and I see a twinkle as a ring in her belly button catches the light.

She has changed so much in the brief time since leaving here. Grown more confident in herself and her abilities.

She is talking to someone on the other end of the line, a boy named Jake. Her cheeks are flushed, and she laughs at something he says, one hip cocked as she fills the kettle. A lover, or a beau, perhaps.

I should be happy for her. Should ask her about him, maybe even invite him out to the croft for dinner so I can meet him. Gauge if he is good enough for my sister. After all, not everyone is so fortunate as to forge their paths when it comes to relationships. Instead, I am flooded with envy that she has what I no longer do.

She hands me the earthen clay mug, and I take it, inhaling the minty, wintergreen scent of willow bark.

"Thanks." I take a sip of the hot drink. It burns my tongue, so I cup it in both hands on my lap until it cools. "Who's Jake?" I nod at the phone, now in her back pocket, for emphasis.

She grins. "Oh, he's great. We met at work. He's in finance. Smart, but so down to earth. When he put his mineral can in the recycle bin instead of the rubbish one after our first date, that's when I knew he was the one."

So, a beau, then. I was right. The stab of envy digs a little deeper.

She's rattling on about how they've been talking about moving in together and she's planning on bringing him to meet me at Samhain. I'm hardly listening, my mind drifting back to Lir and I's first date.

It hadn't been special, or expensive, just a simple day on the beach. We'd swum in the ocean until our skin was like raisins and our eyes burned from the salt, then emerged, laughing and dripping water, to a picnic that he'd packed laid out on a towel. But to me, it had been the most magical thing that anyone had ever done for me.

Arleen must sense my distraction, because she stops talking and looks at me, face contrite. "I'm sorry. Here I am going on and on about how great my life is when you've just lost..." She breaks off and leans forward, putting a hand on my knee. "Listen, I told my boss that I might need to take an extended leave. I can stay here with you for as long as you need."

It's a generous offer and one that I know how much it costs her to make. Arleen is like my father, too soft for this kind of wild living. In truth, I could use some more help around here. I lost a lot of time mourning these past couple of weeks, and midsummer is fast approaching. Rush

41

is a hard worker, maybe the best I've ever seen, but even he can't keep up with everything on his own. I'm normally the one who shears the wool, dyes it, and spins it to sell as yarn at the village market, who picks the apples and boils them until they are soft then puts them in jars so that we will have plenty of preserves come fall, who coaxes the bees from their hives to harvest the fresh honeycomb and tends to the heather garden, leaving the more heavy-duty chores for him.

But the envy growing inside of me has bloomed into a hot, razor-edged thing that cuts me open and leaves me raw and wounded, and I suddenly want to be as far from my sister and her picture-perfect life as I can get.

"Don't be silly. I'm fine. You're still new at this job. You can't afford to take time off, and I won't ask you to put your whole life on hold for me. Besides, I have Rush here to help me. You'd just be in the way."

My words have the desired effect. Arleen sits back, her mouth turning down. Her lips tremble slightly as if I struck her. "Oh. Well, okay then. You-you're probably right. I do have a big meeting Monday that I'm supposed to present at, so it's for the best anyway. I'll just turn in and head back first thing tomorrow morning."

She rises, smoothing out imaginary creases in her pants. She glances at me as she passes, and pauses, worrying her lower lip between her teeth. "I love you, Clare."

I don't respond, only stare into the reddish-brown liquid in my mug, until she's in the bed, under the quilt, and the soft sound of her snores fills the cabin.

8
The Letter

I wave Arleen off the next morning as Rush drives her to the train station, sunlight dancing in her hair, the straight copper strands several shades darker than mine. She doesn't look back as the cart disappears over the first of the green hills, and I don't blame her. I have effectively chased her away. Still, she forgives easily and forgets swiftly. She will be back by the summer solstice.

I collect the mail from the box next to the gate while I'm down there. It is full to overflowing from days of not checking it. Mostly advertisements for cable television and coupons for the grocery that I will never use. There is a letter too, though, wedged between a rolled-up newspaper and the monthly almanac, as if the mail carrier had hastily shoved it inside, not wanting to linger in front of my house any longer than was necessary. I pry it free, turn it over in my hands, and study the fine white stock of the envelope. There is no return address, only a wax seal in the shape of a lion, but I already know who it is from before I open it.

Miss Sage,

I hope this letter finds you in good spirits. I heard of the recent loss of your fiancé from the inspector, and I send my heartfelt condolences. I am writing to you today regarding our recent correspondence about your croft. As someone whose family has ruled over this parish for decades, I understand your desire not to sell your generational home. However, as a businessman, I do hope you realize that I cannot let such a fine plot of land go so easily.

I don't think I am telling you anything you don't know when I say that you own a plot of the most fertile farmland this side of Dublin. Therefore, I would like to make a proposal. Of a partnership, of sorts, between your house and mine. My son, Cairn, is of marrying age, and a fine young man with a penchant for the outdoors. If you and he were to wed, it would give me a piece of your holdings without requiring you to relinquish anything.

I do not expect your answer now. I understand such a decision is not to be made lightly. Think it over, and in one week's time, I will send my son to collect your reply. However, I trust that you will see this as your best option to avoid any conflict.

Yours sincerely,
Lord Geoffrey O'Brian

I stare at the letter until the sun is high in the noonday sky and the words are burned into my retinas, then crumple it in my fist. Geoffrey O'Brian, the fat lord with a runny nose and ruddy cheeks, has long coveted the slice of moorland that sits neatly in my family's name, protected by a piece of paper kept safe in a lock box at a bank in Galway that I have never seen. Over the years, he has tried bribery and threats. Once, he even poisoned the well, though I was never able to prove it was him. I had a tough time saving the crops that year, though I managed, and I lost two ewes that had been around since my mother was a little girl.

Now, it seems, he has resorted to bartering off his own flesh and blood to further line his pockets. I would almost feel sorry for the lad was he not obviously a younger version of his weasel of a father, to agree to go along with such a plan.

Anger brews like an oncoming storm beneath my skin as I storm back up the driveway, not bothering to

44

watch where I'm going. When I stub my toe on a rock, I curse, hopping up and down and clutching the sore appendage, before snatching up the offending bit of hard earth. Rearing back my arm, I start to fling it over the fence and into the road. Maybe the stuffed-shirt lord-to-be's horse will throw a shoe stepping on it. Only something dark catches my attention out of the corner of my eye, and I stop, bringing the stone back for a closer look.

I run my finger across the odd substance that makes an almost starburst pattern across the rock's surface, where years of erosion and wagon wheels have worn it flat. It looks black, at first, though when I hold it up to catch the light, I realize it's a deep, rust red.

Like blood.

The wind rustles the hair on the back of my neck, the sound almost a whisper of my name. Something turns in my stomach as I stare at what I have found, a sick kind of feeling, as if I've eaten something sour. I tell myself I am being silly. The stain on the rock could be anything: a scuff, clay. Why, just last week, I had dropped a jar of jam almost right where I was standing on the way to load it up for the market. And even if it was blood, there was no reason to think it belonged to anything other than one of the pests Nimbus was always chasing around the croft.

Except that Lir was missing, pronounced dead, and this was the last place he was seen alive.

Before I can talk myself out of it, I pocket the stone in my apron before heading back inside, ready to do away with the letter. Still, I hesitate before throwing the letter into the stove when I return to the house, thinking again about all the work that still needs to be done for the harvest before the end of summer. Geoffrey wrote that his son was the outdoorsy type. While it is difficult for me to picture a young lord bent over in a field, his sleeves rolled up and

45

sweat dotting his brow, I cannot deny the extra set of hands, no matter how delicate and lily white they may be, would be useful in the coming days. At the very least, it would show him what real wild crofting life was like and send him running home to his father and their manor full of servants with his tail tucked between his legs.

In the end, I stuff the letter in the pocket of my apron alongside the rock until I have time to examine them further. Then grabbing the wooden bucket off the floor by the sink, I head out to the chicken coop to collect the eggs before they get fertilized.

9

One Isn't Like the Rest

D'arcy calls me two days later, on the new phone that my sister made sure to buy me and had Rush install before she left.

I am baking when it rings, my hands dusted with flour. The oven in the small cast iron stove blazes, turning the room a sweltering degree, and I have opened all of the doors and windows to keep from suffocating. The smells of suet and cinnamon are redolent in the air. A fly buzzes in, circling before attempting to land on one of the seven plates of meat pies cooling on the counter—five for the matron at the orphanage, a charitable donation, and twelve for the confectionary, who pays me by the dozen.

When I want to get my mind off something, I bake.

I already know why he is calling and slide the last two pies for mine and Rush's dinner on the wooden paddle into the flames. Dusting off my hands, I answer it. "Hello?"

"We missed you at the reading of the will today." His voice is both melancholy and accusatory. I can almost see the little wrinkle between his eyebrows that shows up when something is bothering him.

I blow a damp curl off my forehead. "I know. I'm sorry, but I couldn't come sit in a dim, dark room and listen to some wig in a suit read Lir's final wishes from a piece of paper. I just… I couldn't."

"I understand." He pauses, long enough that I think we lost the connection. "He left you his writings and his flat in Galway."

It feels like he has punched me in the gut. "He-he did? What did he leave you?"

"Some of his belongings, stuff he never took with him when he moved out of our parents' house. Will you-will you come over and help me box them up? Mum and Dad are going out of town tomorrow for an extended holiday with Jack, and they want to have everything wrapped up before they leave."

The tears that are becoming as familiar to me as the sound of my voice prick my eyes, and I open my mouth to tell him no. We can't possibly do this now. It's too soon! Only before the words can come, I pull them back.

Putting this off won't change anything or make Lir come back. Better to get it done soon, and quickly, like ripping off a bandage, than draw out the pain.

"Sure."

I wait for the pies to finish cooking then wrap up the ones to take into town in a basket along with mine. I will eat it while I ride. The last one I leave on the windowsill to cool.

I find Rush in the barn, mucking out the stalls. I tell him where I am going as I saddle Rhiannon and that I'm not sure what time I'll be home, but that there is a meat pie inside plus leftover flag salad in the icebox if he gets hungry.

"Do you want me to come with you?" he asks, and I weigh the merit of accepting his offer. Having him there for support would be nice. In the time that he has come to stay here, we have become close, in the way that two coworkers sharing a cubicle in an office might. But his relationship with Lir hadn't been what you would call good.

He was their family's groundskeeper before Lir caught him stealing his mother's jewels and got him fired. While I didn't think that Rush harbored him any ill will—

"What's fair is fair," he would say whenever the subject came up—what D'arcy and I were going to be doing was personal. Private.

"No thanks. I'll be fine."

"Okay." He turns back to his work. "Be careful."

"I will." I leave, leading Rhiannon out by the halter.

It doesn't take me long to deliver the pies and then travel the short distance to the Flynns' home. D'arcy is waiting for me in the front yard. He helps me dismount, leaving Rhiannon free to graze inside the fenced-in property before we walk indoors.

The rest of his family isn't here. Probably they're still at the lawyer's, signing a mountain of paperwork, or else at the post office, setting up their mail to forward to wherever they're going. I am glad. I don't want to face them right now, don't want to try and explain why their son left me his two most valuable possessions. I feel like I have stolen something from them, although I never asked Lir for anything other than his love.

I know the steps to his old room by heart. I could have counted them in my sleep, right down to the creaky floorboard in the middle of the hallway between his room and the bathroom. My heart aches at the hours we spent here as kids, and then as teenagers, running up and down the stairs as his mom yelled for us to slow down, playing hide and seek in the cupboards, staying up late watching movies and eating popcorn until our eyes were heavy and our fingers greasy with butter.

D'arcy turns on the light.

Right away, I can tell nothing has been touched.

Mrs. Flynn had insisted that the room be kept ready for Lir in the event he wanted to stay the night when he came home for the holidays, though he usually wound up staying at my place. After he went missing, she became

49

even more adamant about the room not being touched, as if keeping her son's childhood room the same would ensure he would one day come home to use it. Only now, he never will.

The bed is made neatly, the thick black comforter drawn up over the pillows, the sheets tucked at the corners. The computer in the corner is off, its monitor dark and coated in a thick layer of dust. A mobile made out of small bits of stained glass hangs from the window frame, casting a kaleidoscope of bright blues, sunshine yellows, and deep scarlets across the floor. The tall grandfather clock—the one Lir had gotten at an antique sale for a steal and fixed it up until it worked again, though it still leaned a little to the left—ticks loudly in the quiet. The scent of him, a mixture of mint and lye, covers everything.

I wish I didn't have to breathe.

D'arcy drags a stack of cardboard boxes in from the hallway. "Here." He hands me three. "Put his entertainment stuff in these. I'll do his clothes."

"Okay." I take the boxes, wondering how so much of a person's life can fit into such a small space, and make myself move farther into the room. The air is cold, causing goose bumps to sprout along my arms. A glance at the vent in the corner reveals the air isn't on.

The shelf, where a younger Lir had kept his CDs, books, and movies, is covered in cobwebs. I take each one down, praying no arachnids are hiding in the small, dark corners, and lay them carefully in the boxes. A few of the leatherbound volumes I pause over and run my hands lovingly along the covers.

Burns. Shaw. Wilde.

These were his favorites, the poets, authors, and playwrights he'd devoured repeatedly, whose works had eventually made him want to become a writer.

50

The wastebasket next to the desk is full of wadded-up papers. Several of them roll out onto the floor when I upend the can into a trash bag. I scramble after them on hands and knees, picking them back up. As I do, I realize that one of them isn't made of notebook paper like the rest.

Curious, I sit back on my haunches and unroll it.

It is a picture. The same picture, in fact, of Lir and I that I had found stuck under my jewelry box the day of his memorial. I frown, staring at it. Why would it be tossed out with the rubbish? Had Lir done it in a fit of rage after one of our spats, then forgotten to take it back out? Or had someone else thrown it away, either accidentally or on purpose? And if so, who?

Unable to answer any of my questions, I smooth the picture out as best I can and lay it in the box with the rest of the stuff.

D'arcy notices, well-trained eyes missing nothing. "What's that?"

"Just an old picture."

Not dissuaded, he picks it up and studies it, the corners of his mouth turned down slightly. "This is of you and Lir. Who would have put it in the trash? Did the two of you have a fight?"

It is the same thing I asked myself moments ago, and I shake my head. "No more than any other couple." I can practically see the wheels in his head turning as he mulls this over. "What are you thinking?"

"That maybe someone other than my brother threw it away."

"It's possible, I guess. But who else would have had access to this room?"

"Only my family and Rush. I remember running into him in the hall upstairs the day he was leaving and thinking it was odd. He said he was using the loo since the

51

one downstairs was on the fritz, but maybe he never truly got over the fact that Lir had him fired."

"Maybe," I agree, although it is hard for me to imagine someone as gentle-hearted as Rush harming anyone. Then I remember the bloodstained rock I'd found in the driveway, now sitting at the bottom of my jewelry box, and reconsidered. "I thought you eliminated him as a suspect right after Lir went missing, though."

"Because you said he was in the barn all night, yes. However, as far as alibis go, that's a tenuous one at best. It's entirely plausible that he was able to sneak out and return without you noticing."

He tucks the photograph into his pocket, and I know he will take it out again later when he is alone. He will probably even get the old case files out again and spread them across his living room floor. Never mind that he has gone down this rabbit hole once already with no result.

For now, the conversation is closed, although a tiny voice that sounds at once like mine and not mine hisses in the back of my mind to press the subject further. To get the picture for myself and convince D'arcy to let sleeping dogs lie. It will be better for him, it insists. Better for both of us.

I ignore it, and we continue our work in silence, cleaning out Lir's room and packing up his stuff for hours. There is much more in here than I remembered—rowing trophies and wool-darned socks and a package of gum that has long since gone stale. All the kinds of human clutter that people collect during their lives then leave behind for their loved ones to try to decide what to do with it. When we are done, we put all the boxes in the living room by the front door.

D'arcy walks me out, hands shoved deep in his pockets. We talk a little more, about the things we packed up today and the reading, neither quite willing to say good

52

night. Finally, when the sun has all but set below the hills, I give him one last hug and set off for home.

10
Cairn O'Brian, Earl of the Manor at Leinster Shire

I am in the low field, harvesting the honey, when Cairn comes to call, riding over the rolling green hills on a massive black stallion whose coat gleams like ink still wet on the page. The beautiful creature tosses its mane every couple of feet, pulling at the bit, eager to break into a gallop across the grassy moor. The lord's son must be a skilled rider, however, because he reins him in each time with merely a click of his tongue, his free hand resting casually on the pommel of his polished leather saddle.

A dog trots at his side, a flop-eared mastiff nearly half the size of the horse. Its pink tongue lolls from its mouth, panting in the heat of the afternoon. When a hedgehog rustles in the nearby brush, it darts after it, barking excitedly, before being called back to its master's side with a whistle.

Nimbus, who has been dozing in the shade of the hives, leaps to her feet with a hiss, back arching at the sound, and scrambles onto my shoulder, claws digging into the tender flesh beneath my work clothes.

Cairn dismounts in front of me, the buckles on his knee-high boots jingling smartly when he lands. His golden blond hair falls to one side in what is probably meant to be a rakish look, but which I find annoying.

I scowl at him. "I thought your father said seven days. It's only been six."

He flashes me a smile as white and straight as the rest of him. "Forgive me. But the desire to make your acquaintance was too strong for me to resist any longer. Cairn O'Brian, earl of the manor at Leinster Shire and future lord of County Kirk, at your service." He bows at the waist, the long cloak he wears flapping behind him majestically. It is a fine thing, made of thick, dark velvet, and wholly impractical for this kind of weather, worn only to impress. I hope he is sweating like a pig in it.

"The pleasure is all mine." I turn away from him, back to my work, and he straightens, looking taken aback at my abrupt, dismissive tone as if he is unsure what to do next. I suppose he is used to girls swooning at such an introduction. However, I will not be won over so easily.

To his credit, he recovers quickly.

"Here. Let me help you with that." He moves to take the dripping honeycomb from my hands before I can stop him, unconcerned with the bees buzzing around his bare hands.

With grudging admiration, I watch as he carefully breaks it into even squares before dropping them into the cheesecloth-lined jars I have brought with me. His fingers are sticky when he is done. Yet rather than look for something to wipe them on, he licks them clean. His lips make a childish smacking sound that is at once endearing and irritating.

"You have a way with animals," I observe, noting his un-stung palms.

"And you have the finest honey I have ever tasted." He tilts his head toward the softly buzzing hives. "I wonder if I might trouble you for some more, perhaps in a cup of tea?"

"Of course," I acquiesce politely, though the thought of him in my home makes my skin prickle. "Go in and make yourself comfortable. I will stable your horse and be right with you."

55

11
A Marriage of Convenience

I put the stallion in the empty stall next to Rhiannon's, where the horse we had before her used to live until it slipped on a loose piece of shale two rainy seasons ago, broke its leg, and had to be put down, and give it some oats and water before going inside.

Cairn is sitting at the table, cloak draped over the back of his chair. Without it to cover him, I can't help but notice the lean, strong set of his shoulders, and the swan-like elegance of his neck. I busy myself with the kettle so that he won't see the traitorous heat creeping up my collarbone. It has been a long time since I have been alone with a man, not counting Rush, who is like a brother to me. Not since the last time I saw Lir. Apparently, my body hasn't forgotten its natural urges.

The brutish beast lays at his feet, drool oozing from its jowls to pool in a puddle on the floor. I wince at the thought of having to mop it up later.

"Can't you do something with that thing?" I point at the dog so he knows what I'm talking about.

He follows the line of my finger with raised eyebrows. "Who, Mastodon? Don't worry. He's completely harmless."

Nimbus slashes the air with her claws as if protesting this statement, from her perch atop my shoulder. Mastodon lifts his head, a growl rumbling low in his throat, but stays where he is.

I put my hands on my hips. "He's making a mess all over my clean floor, not to mention agitating my cat. Either you put him outside, or I will." I call a small tornado, just enough that he can see the air swirling above my palm, to make my point, and he sits up straighter, eyes wide. Except he doesn't look afraid. More like he's intrigued by my show of power.

"Mas, out." He says the dog's name, a simple, firm command, and the animal gets to its feet and trots outside, wedging its nose in the crack between the door and the jamb to open it.

"Thank you."

I pour the tea, hands empty of magic once more, and hand him a cup, keeping the other for myself. Still, there is a modicum of respect in his gaze that wasn't there before as he watches me sit across from him.

"I've always wondered if the rumors about your power were as true as the villagers make them out to be."

I lift an eyebrow. Nimbus hops down and curls onto my lap, content now that the dog is gone, and I stroke her back with one hand. "And is your curiosity satisfied?"

"Amply." He stirs his tea, mixing in the honey, but makes no move to drink it. He is awkward again, posture hunching slightly, and I know he is trying to find the right words to say what he must say next, the tea nothing but a convenient ruse to open the conversation to what he came here for.

After a minute, he clears his throat and begins.

"I don't think it's any secret that my father covets your land and wishes for us to marry so that our family can claim joint ownership of it."

The direct approach it is, then.

I take a long drink of my tea, peering at him over the rim. "And what makes you think that I will so readily accept such an offer?"

"Look, I know what you have been through recently, with your fiancé being pronounced dead."

57

He reaches for my hand, the movement too personal, too intimate for someone I hardly know, and I flinch at the mention of Lir's name, lip curling.

"You have no idea what I have been through." The words are venom from my lips. "What have you ever lost that you genuinely cared about, had taken from you that you did not wish to keep? You bluebloods are all the same, sitting neat and pretty in your cozy homes, pretending like you understand your constituents because you deign to visit the market and mingle with the commoners or attend a barn raising or sit at a sickbed now and then. But you have no idea how hard life can be out here, the kind of harsh things it makes you face."

He drops his fingers, properly abashed. Yet his chin remains lifted. "You're right. I don't. I have never wanted for anything in my life save one thing: my freedom. In this, I still think we might help each other."

I fold my arms, unwilling to hear him out while also intrigued at what he might say next. "And how is that, pray tell?"

"Simple." He mimics my body language. "I wish to be out from under my father's thumb. You wish to keep your croft running." One corner of his mouth snakes up at my look of surprise. "It doesn't take a genius to notice the fence along the road is in desperate need of repair, or that you're almost a month late in the season to be collecting honey. We don't have to make it anything that it's not."

I rub my thumb over my palm, where a scar I don't remember getting runs a rough, jagged line over my calluses, pondering his words. "You're proposing a marriage of convenience."

"Why not? This way, we both get what we need, and my father is satisfied at the same time. Besides, be honest." He fixes me with a look that is at once electrifying

58

and chilling. "What do you have to lose?"

My home if I say no, I think. My dignity, or what's left of it, if I say yes. But I say none of this out loud. For a moment, the sight before me shimmers and changes, until it is no longer Cairn sitting in front of me holding but Lir. His hair is long, overdue for a haircut because he's so busy with his studies, and pulled back in a low ponytail at the base of his neck. One thick curl has sprung free and falls forward into his eyes, giving him an unkempt, boyish look that reminds me of our school days. He smiles at me, one side of his mouth curving up before the other like it always has.

"Marry me, Clare," he whispers and holds out a ring to slip on my finger.

Ignoring the frantic pulse in my wrists, I brush it aside like cobwebs and stretch my hand out across the table to him. "Deal. On one condition."

"Name it."

"You don't hunt the rabbits. You and your dog can track any other game you like, but they are sacred to my family, especially the large golden one with blue eyes. The fluffle must be left alone, for killing them would have a disastrous effect upon my abilities."

He doesn't even take a minute to think it over, but instead reaches out and takes my hand. His fingers are warm in mine. "As you wish it, so shall it be."

12

A Butterscotch

I had always known Lir and I were from different worlds, in the way that a child knows the grass is green and the sky is blue. His family's house was a fine brick Tudor, with so many rooms that the first time I saw it, I was sure they couldn't possibly use them all. They had electricity instead of candles and running water instead of a well. The stove ran on gas, as did the fireplace, and machines that rumbled like sleeping monsters washed their dishes and laundry.

Even his clothes had an aura of newness that mine did not—polished shoes with unfettered laces, pants without holes, shirts pressed with an iron and labeled with all of the latest brands. My homespun dresses and worn work boots looked positively threadbare in comparison.

He always had the money for a hot lunch served by the school cafeteria and soda pop from the vending machine, whereas I was forced to bring brown bag sandwiches from home and drink my water from the free fountain. But what all that meant didn't become apparent until one market day.

We were thirteen. My mother, sister, and I had driven the cart into town like we did the first Saturday of every month. We set up shop at the end of the street, far enough away from the other vendors that they would not feel threatened by us but close enough to attract customers.

Our wares we displayed on a deep blue and white checkered cloth in the back of the cart: sticks of freshly churned butter wrapped in wax paper, bundles of dried herbs, sticks of firewood stacked haphazardly on top of one another. We stayed all day, my mother haggling over fair prices with each new buyer while my sister, Lir, and I played tag in the dirt. Once the last customer had trickled home, we gathered what little coin we had made and went across the street to the small grocery to purchase the few necessities the croft could not provide. Toilet paper in soft white rolls, gunny sacks of flour and sugar, oil for the lamp.

As always, Arleen and I couldn't help but stop and stare at the colorful sweets situated in neat little glass jars behind the counter. Ribbon candies. Peppermint pieces. Sour lemon drops. Chewy caramels. Chocolate bars bigger than my hand, and lollipops in every flavor you could imagine.

We knew better than to ask for any. Candy was a luxury we couldn't afford. Still, we couldn't help but linger over the delectable display cases as the clerk rang up our purchases and my mama counted out the coins from her purse. It wasn't until I'd started to turn away that I saw it.

The edge of a bright yellow plastic wrapper peeked out from under the counter. It gleamed in the light streaming in through the plate glass display windows, like a drop of sunlight made solid.

A butterscotch.

It must have fallen out of the jar unnoticed, and my heart skipped a beat. Surely no one would care about one dirty candy that was no longer good to sell. Like the rubbish in the alley bins that the mangy curs who roamed the outskirts of the village got into, loved by no one but tolerated by all, snapping and snarling at each other over the last bone or a scrap of meat. This was something I could have.

I reached for it, going down on grubby hands and knobby knees to pull it out of its hiding place. I felt a flash of guilt that there was not enough to share with my sister.

61

However, my childhood longing quickly overshadowed any mature thoughts of giving away my find.

The paper crinkled as I unwrapped it and popped it in my mouth. Rich, buttery flavor, followed by a river of sugar, exploded across my tongue. I was sure I had never tasted anything quite as delicious, nor ever would again, and I sucked on the candy, savoring it as long as I could.

"Hey! Gobdaw, little moor trash. You better be able to pay for that."

The expletive caught me off guard and rooted me in place as the elderly man behind the cash register pointed at the offending empty wrapper in my hand. A scowl painted his lips downward, carving deep canyons in the lines of his face. My mother turned, following his gaze. I watched her face fall when she realized what I had done, and felt my stomach follow it to the floor as I recognized the look in her eyes. We did not have the money to pay for it.

I wanted to tell them that I hadn't stolen it. That it had been going to go in the trash anyway, so what difference did it make if I'd eaten it? Only my tongue seemed to have gotten stuck to the roof of my mouth, and I couldn't form the words.

Not that it mattered. I could tell by the clerk's expression that he wouldn't believe me. And even if my mum did, there was a good chance he wouldn't listen to her either.

Visions of cold jail cells, military camps, and schools for delinquents—all of the places Lir had told me that grownups sent kids who didn't behave—danced through my head. I broke out in a cold sweat. Part of me wanted to run, to escape to the moor. There, I could hide among the wild fairy mounds in the hidden places where they would never find me until they gave up the search. But I knew that would only make me look guiltier.

My fate hung over my head like an executioner's blade as my mother turned back to the man. Resignation lined every inch of her body, making her seem to wilt.

Before she could speak, Lir stepped forward and pressed a folded bill into her hand. "Excuse me, Ms. Sage. I think you dropped this."

My mother blinked away tears but didn't argue as she thanked him and paid the clerk for the candy.

His frown deepened as he looked from Lir to me to my mother before giving a sharp nod. He pushed the keys harder than was normal, shoved the cash into the drawer, then reluctantly counted out her change. We all knew the money was Lir's. Though, the older man wasn't going to split hairs, so long as he got paid.

I spit the candy in the waste basket on the way out the door. The taste had soured in my mouth, making me feel nauseous.

I never ate another piece after that day. And while we never talked about it, my mother never forgot what Lir did for us. Up until the day she died, she had something special made for him when he came over. Cookies. A sweater. New socks.

I didn't forget either.

The man hadn't questioned Lir, although he had been lying. Whereas I was presumed guilty without hesitation. Not because of the money, though that was certainly part of it. Even then, I understood that money spoke in ways words couldn't. Because he was the son of a respectable banker, a member of the community. While I was the daughter of the moor witch, an outsider. Someone different. Other.

And even if I was grateful for the way Lir had saved me, and I was, after that day, a tiny part of me resented him for belonging in a place where I did not, and never would.

13
Stop Acting Like a Big Ninny

"You're getting married?" My sister's voice through the phone line is a shrill scream that makes me wince. I can almost hear her jumping up and down on the other end, like an out-of-control wind-up monkey.

"Arleen, please." I raise my voice enough that she can hear me over her squeals. "It's not a big deal. Yes, I'm getting married. But like I said, it's only to save the farm from falling into complete ruin, not to mention the hands of someone outside our bloodline. Cairn and I have struck a deal. Although in order to pull it off before his father changes his mind, I'm going to need your help. Will you be my maid of honor?"

"Your maid of honor?" Arleen screams even louder than before and claps her hands. Somehow, she manages not to drop her cell.

"Well, only if you stop acting like a big ninny."

"Sorry. I'm just so surprised! In a good way, though. I mean, I always thought…" She breaks off, but it's too late. I already know what she was going to say. That she thought I would wed Lir, like everyone else in the village had since we were two inseparable kids chasing fireflies across the moor. The reminder is like a railroad spike being driven through my chest, and I have to force myself to remember how to breathe past the pain. "Never mind. Of course, I'll help you. When is the big day?"

"Two weeks from Sunday."

"Two weeks?" And we're back to the shrieking.

"That leaves us barely any time at all! I'll have to put in another request for time off form and come straight down tomorrow. If I call the station now, I'm sure I can still get a ticket. We'll do the dress first, then the food and flowers, plus any other decorations."

There is a scrambling noise, followed by the rustle of paper and pencil as she makes a list, and I sit back in my chair, only half-listening and nodding obediently as she rattles off instructions for appointments I need to make before she arrives.

14
Another of Those Things I Needed to Do Alone

"So, is it true?" D'arcy asks the question without any of the dramatics Arleen had exhibited as he lets me into his small cottage. I came right over after getting off the phone with my sister to tell him the news. Yet it seems that the news has already spread through the village gossip vine like wildfire. Still, it feels fitting that he should hear it from me as well, seeing how his brother, were he still alive, would have been the groom if things had gone as planned.

Rush had offered to come with me again, after extending his congratulations on my upcoming nuptials, but I turned him down. This is another of those things I needed to do alone.

There seem to be a lot more of them lately.

D'arcy closes the door behind me. His voice is flat and emotionless, filled with gravel that scrapes at my skin. He's been drinking, whiskey judging by the bottle next to the half-empty glass on the sideboard next to the scattered mess of case files, witness reports, and grainy crime scene photos. The guilt of not being able to solve his brother's disappearance eating away at him.

"Are you really marrying Cairn, then?"

"Yes," I admit. "But it's not what you think. It's a marriage of convenience."

"Convenient." He snorts. "That's one word for it."

"What do you mean?"

"Nothing. It's just—" He runs a hand through his hair, clearly agitated about something. "Don't you think it's at least a little suspicious that barely a month after Lir is pronounced dead, Lord O'Brian happens to come up with the idea for you to marry his son?"

"Like what, he killed Lir so that he could get half the rights to my land through marriage?" I mean it as a joke, yet no sooner have the words left my mouth than a shiver runs down my spine when I recall the almost vision-like memory that I'd had of Lir yesterday when Cairn proposed. Was this the message my mind had been trying to send?

D'arcy waves the words away as soon as they leave my mouth. "You're right. It's preposterous. Still, I can't get rid of this nagging feeling in the back of my head that I'm missing something. Something obvious that I should have seen earlier. Only for the life of me, I don't know what." He picks up the glass and downs the rest of his drink in one gulp, breathing a little heavily when he sits it back down, the alcohol rushing through his bloodstream. "Lir would have been happy for you."

It is not at all what I expect him to say next, and I give him my full attention, forehead furrowing. "How can you know that?"

He turns his head sideways enough to meet my gaze, eyes glittering in the dimly lit sitting room the same way Lir's used to whenever we were discussing something important. My heart gives a heavy thump in my chest that is not unlike a stone falling into a well. How I wish he was here. "Because he wouldn't want you to stop living your life simply because his is over. This is a good thing, Clare. It's good for you. Cairn will be good for you, for the croft."

I'm not sure whether he is trying to convince me, himself, his dead twin, or all three of us.

"I know." I sigh, looking down at my hands, where my fingers have twisted themselves into the laces of my dress.

D'arcy watches me knowingly. "But?"

I am quiet as I think of how to word my answer so that he will understand. Ever the inspector, D'arcy waits patiently, no poking or prodding, as if he senses how hard this is for me. Finally, I lift my eyes back to his. His face swims through my tears. "But he's not the one I was meant to be with."

"You mean Lir." It is not a question.

I nod anyway. My voice seems to have fled the coop.

"Listen to me, Clare." D'arcy takes my hand. His skin is warm from the booze and the unaired house. "Lir loved you and you loved him. Everyone knows that. Maybe, before all this happened, you were meant to be together, but fate changed. He's gone now. You have to accept that. You have to move on. We all do."

"That's rich advice, coming from someone who is still trying to solve a cold case behind his captain's back." The first tendrils of anger leak into my voice as I sweep a hand at the documents he was studying before I arrived. "Besides, what if I can't? What if I don't want to? What if letting Lir go and moving on with my life means forgetting him, and that's something I'm not willing to do?"

"It's not." D'arcy's fingers tighten around mine, strong, insistent. "You never have to forget Lir or the time you shared. But you can get on with your life for yourself, Clare, for Lir. At the very least, because wherever he is, he deserves to know that you're okay."

I glare at him and open my mouth to disagree. To tell him that he can do whatever he likes, but I have no desire to replace his brother's place in my heart by kindling any kind of romance with Cairn. That this contract between us is strictly business, nothing else. Except when I blink, the person in front of me isn't D'arcy anymore, but Lir. He is holding my hand tightly, nails biting into my skin, his face inches from mine. His eyes are hard as flint.

"Don't do it, Clare," he whispers. "Don't marry him."

I snatch my hand away, a gasp tearing out of my throat, and the image of Lir shatters like a broken mirror. It is once again D'arcy and I standing there, alone. Briefly, I wonder if my exhaustion from the stress of the past few weeks has finally caught up with me, and I dozed off. Only the fresh sheen of sweat on my skin that has nothing to do with the heat of the evening remains, letting me know it wasn't a dream.

D'arcy watches me, concern lining the corners of his face. "Clare, are you okay?" He starts to touch my forehead, the way my mom would when I was younger and she was checking to see if I had a fever.

I jerk back from his touch, not wanting to risk seeing something else that isn't there. "I'm fine," I snap, knowing my voice sounds harsh but unable to help it. My hands shake where the mirage of Lir held them. My mind is a chaos of questions I don't have the answers to—why do I keep seeing these things? Is it my conscience trying to tell me that I'm making a mistake by marrying Cairn? Or is it something else? "I'm tired, that's all. I should go." I walk to the door and out onto the porch before he can protest.

D'arcy follows hands up in surrender. "I'm sorry, Clare. Please. I didn't mean to... Forget about it. Do me a favor, though, and think about what I said, all right? About Cairn and the wedding. Don't throw this opportunity away."

"I'm not." I set my chin, pushing all thoughts of Lir and the way his fake image—the only logical explanation for what I saw—had looked at me as far away as I can. "I accepted Cairn's proposal to save the croft, and I will see it through. I don't need you, or anyone else, to tell me what to

69

do with my life beyond that."

D'arcy touches my bare arm gently, scared to get too close to me now, as if I am a wildcat that will hiss and scratch at him. When I don't, he gives me a small, sad smile. "I understand."

"I know."

We stay there for a long minute, as daylight fades to twilight above the tall oaks. Then, without another parting word, I descend the stairs, mount my horse, and head home to prepare for my sister's arrival.

15
The Library

I am halfway back to the cottage when I change my mind and turn around, riding to the library instead. It is raining when I get there. I tie Rhiannon to the low-hanging branch of a tree on the lawn and stand there a moment, waiting to see if the downpour will lessen.

The wind tossed the boughs over our heads, scattering leaves at my feet as she grazed. Busts in the shape of crows perch on the eaves above the windows, water pouring from the spouts in their open beaks. Though I know they are not real, the statues appear to watch me, stone eyes cast in shadow thanks to the dark and cloudy weather. I shiver, casting a last glance at the sky, and sprint through the rain and up the stairs into the large brick building.

The heavy double doors slam shut behind me, echoing through the empty silence. I stand in the foyer for a minute, arms wrapped around my middle, dripping water onto the black and white marble floor, before making my way into the stacks.

I am not sure exactly what it is I'm looking for until I find myself in the poetry aisle. My eyes go immediately to the slender gold-embossed volume bearing Lir's name, and I pull it off the shelf, running my fingers tenderly over the letters. I open it, reading the poems he published in our final year of school, lips moving as silent as the grave. They were all ones he had written about me and then kept hidden away in a spiral notebook for years, until I discovered them one afternoon while we were doing homework together and convinced him to send them in.

They had gotten him his scholarship to university.

Her hair was long and full of grace
Brushing, feather-like, against her face.

Lips as full and red as the rose
Formed a murmur of words no one would ever
know.

Words that are not from the books that she reads,
But words from the heart that inside of her bleeds.

Still, she is beautiful,
my Ophelia immortal.

Tears prick my eyes, staining the paper a mottled gray, and I turn the pages with a sniff. A footfall redirects my attention from the chapbook, my heartbeat kicking up at the sound. I hadn't expected anyone to be in here this late, though the library was open twenty-four-seven. I suppose it is not unheard of for a student from the local school to be studying at night. Or perhaps the librarian had stayed over to do some overdue shelving.

"Hello?" My voice echoes through the wide antechamber. "Is someone there?"

There is no reply at first, and I begin to think I imagined the noise. Then there is an unmistakable cough, followed by the shuffling of footsteps from the other side of the stack in front of me, and I know I did not.

I peer through the books on the shelf, trying to see who is standing on the other side. I can make out the shape of a shadowy form, and I squint, wishing that the lanterns hung at the end of each row were a little brighter.

Thump!

A book falls off the shelf a few feet away from where I stand, and I jump. I stare at it, heart jack rabbiting, with a frown, wondering what had knocked it off the shelf. Perhaps the person on the other side? Before I can bend to pick it up and replace it, another one falls, then another, and another.

Thump! Thump! Thump!

Books fly off the shelf in a steady stream as if they are being thrown by an invisible hand, pages rustling, spines flapping, heading right for the spot where I stand. I stumble back, tripping over a stool, and fall with a scream, landing hard on my rear. Books pelt me from all sides, their bindings nicking my bare arms, and I scramble to my feet, wet shoes slipping and squeaking on the floor. My heart is in my throat. I taste the iron tang of blood from where I bit my tongue. I can hardly believe this is happening.

Someone is shouting my name, the voice like a great howling wind, and I cover my ears, doing my best to protect my face and eyes from the attacking books as I run from the room without looking back.

Thunder booms and lightning flashes, inches from striking the tree where Rhiannon waits as I dash across the lawn. I don't stop as I rip her reins free from the tree hard enough to snap the branch and jump onto her back. I kick my heels into her sides, and she responds, tossing her head with a whinny before leaping into a gallop.

I don't dare a glance over my shoulder until we have reached the end of the road. When I do, I see that the library doors are still open, and what looks like a person is standing beneath the archway. I shield my eyes with one hand, trying to make out who it is through the rain. But another lightning bolt flashes, blinding me. When it clears, the doorway is empty, leaving me to wonder if anyone had ever been there at all, or if I'd imagined the whole thing.

73

Only the cuts on my arms, which I treated and bandaged when I got home with a tincture of meadowsweet that would have them fade in a day and avoid any awkward questions, told me that I hadn't.

16

A Bad Dream

"Clare." Lir's voice is like a soft summer breeze rolling off the waves. His arms encircle me from behind, holding me against his lean, powerful chest. I close my eyes and listen to the rhythmic beating of his heart. "Promise me something."

"Anything," I whisper, and I mean it. I will give him whatever he asks for, even if it is my soul. That is how much I love him.

His lips brush my hair, tickling my ear. "Promise me that you'll always be mine."

What a silly request. I almost chuckle, amused and a bit confused that he even needs to ask. We both know I could never be anyone else's. Have never been anyone else's. "I promise."

"Clare." Lir's voice changes, becoming harsher, more grating, like icicles scraping against a window. I turn to look at him, to ask if he is feeling all right. But the words fly off my tongue like ashes on the wind. My eyes widen, filling with horror, as I struggled to understand what I am seeing.

Lir's face, his beautiful face, is caved in from the back, as if he has been struck in the head with a heavy object. One of his eyeballs dangles from its socket. Blood drips onto my overalls, and I wheeze, my throat too tight to scream, as I struggle to break free of his vice-like grip.

Empty spaces where several of his teeth have rotted out gape at me as he opens his lips in a snarl, and I think I see bugs swarming at the back of his mouth, filling his throat. "You lied."

"No!"

I sit up in bed, gasping for air that won't come. My heart races in my chest like a runaway horse, and my hands tremble when I bury them in my hair. They come away soaked with what, for a horrible moment, I think is blood. Have I been struck on the head, too? Was D'arcy right, and Cairn killed Lir, then snuck back here to finish the job while I slept?

I nearly fall out of bed in my haste to light the lamp, certain I will see a shadowy figure standing in the corner, an ax or other blunt-edged weapon in his hands. Yet the cabin is empty, and when I hold my fingers up to the light, relief floods through me. It is merely sweat.

Bile rises in my throat as I remember the buzzing insects swarming in Lir's mouth, and I barely make it to the edge of the mattress before I throw up. Nimbus lifts her head from the small nest she has made in the quilt and blinks accusingly at me. Her fur is ruffled from sleep.

"Sorry, girl." I stroke her back with trembling fingers, trying to make my voice sound reassuring. "I didn't mean to wake you. I had a bad dream, that's all."

She purrs and butts my palm, letting me know that I am forgiven.

I clean up the mess I made and wash my hands in the basin until they are raw and clean. Unfortunately, no amount of scrubbing is going to remove the yellow puke stain on my night dress. I remove it, throw it away, and change into a fresh one, then flop back down on my pillows, trying to get comfortable again. But peace alludes me, the vision of Lir's ghost, or apparition, or spirit, or whatever the bloody hell that thing was supposed to be reappearing on the backs of my eyelids every time I start to drift off. Finally, I get up again, careful not to disturb my pet for a second time, and busy myself with making an

76

early breakfast instead.

17

My Best Option

"Oh, Clare, it's gorgeous!" my sister enthuses, circling me as I stand in front of the three-way mirror in the dress maker's shop on the corner of Maple and Elm. "This is the one. Can you maybe sew it a little tighter at the hips, though?"

The older woman nods, her mouth full of pins. She begins to make the necessary alterations at once, tugging and pinching at the fabric so hard it makes me wobble.

I have to admit, I think, studying my reflection, Arleen is right. The gown is beautiful, a long, white cotton thing with gossamer off-the-shoulder straps. I should be overflowing with joy, especially when I take a peek at the price tag. On sale. Yet my skin is a wan, sallow color, and there are dark circles under my eyes from my fitful night's sleep.

"How will you be wearing your hair?"

"Up, I think," I reply, and my sister nods her approval. "It will accent the neckline better." Plus, Lir always preferred my hair down. His wild witch, he would call me, tugging playfully at my curls. After the way my imagination has been running away with itself the past few days, the less I think of him during the ceremony, the better.

"We'll practice when we get home, then. Better to get it right now so you know exactly what you want rather than waiting until the morning of to decide."

"Okay." I don't argue, though the thought of spending more hours being primped until my roots are as sore as my skin where the seamstress keeps accidentally poking me through the fabric is less than appealing. If it were up to me, Cairn and I would go to the courthouse, have the magistrate perform a quick ceremony, and that would be that. No muss, no fuss. After all, what do we have to celebrate?

What would be the point? Arleen has her heart set on my having a traditional wedding as our parents did, and I am sure Lord O'Brian will feel the same way about his only son. Still, some of my reluctance must show on my face, because she frowns.

"Are you sure you like it, Clare? You don't seem—I don't know—as happy as I thought you would be."

The woman at my feet grunts, as if wishing we had said something before she'd made half a dozen holes in the dress. I hesitate, actually considering telling her everything I didn't when she came down for the memorial service— how badly I miss Lir. How a day doesn't go by without him consuming some part of my thoughts. And more—how I have been seeing things, seeing him, when I am awake and asleep. How I'm not sure I ought to be standing here getting ready for a wedding where he is not the groom.

Only I stop myself at the last minute, remind myself that if I don't do this, it will only be a matter of time before I am forced to sell the croft to Lord O'Brian anyway. This is my best option if I want to keep our family home intact.

I smile at her, doing my best to make it look convincing. "Yes, I really do."

18

Who Needs Peripheral Vision, Anyway?

I lay in the tub, submerged up to my neck, my hair piled on top of my head. My sister has stepped outside to help Rush till the field, giving me a few precious moments of privacy that are rarer now that she is here again. A book rests on the metal tray in front of me, illuminated by a few flickering beeswax candles, but I make no move to read it. Instead, I remain still, eyes closed, chest rising and falling steadily. The water is warm, lapping gently at my skin like the tentative touch of a new lover. Unbidden, another memory, of the first time Lir and I slept together, rises to the surface of my mind.

"Clare."

Lir says my name as if it is magic, as if I have put a spell on him that makes him completely and wholly mine, and he pulls me to him until there is no space left between us. He removes my clothes, one garment at a time, kissing each bare place where they fall. A part of me whispers that I shouldn't do this, should make him wait until we are wed, but I have never been able to tell him no and brush away the warning, undressing him as he did me and running my fingers nervously but eagerly over the muscled planes of his chest, the stubbled curve of his jaw, the dip of his hips. He presses his lips to mine, claiming me, and though there is some pain when he slides inside me, it soon settles, and my body fits around him like a glove.

We rock, slow at first, then faster, two waves crashing against one another, as our passion builds to a storm-like crescendo that explodes in a fiery shower strong enough to create new universes and leaves us shuddering, gripping one another as if we are both too afraid to let go.

Tears roll down my face, and I swipe at them furiously, angry at myself for letting them come in the first place. My elbow hits the candle, knocking it into the water, where it douses with a hiss. I climb out of the tub, nearly falling on my face as I attempt to banish the memory. But it refuses to leave as if it has been permanently etched into my mind.

Determined to think about something else, anything else, other than the desire now itching between my thighs, I busy myself with getting dressed, dumping the bath water into the yard, and drying out the tub. By the time Arleen and Rush return to the house for dinner, the rims around my eyes are barely pink, the flush all but gone from my skin.

Yet I do not answer when she asks me how my bath was, pretending not to hear her as I mix greens for a salad. After asking a second time, she gives up. Instead, I remove the bun, letting my hair tumble freely past my face, and use it to hide the emotions still swimming in my eyes, lest either one sees them and guesses the truth behind my silence.

It is something I haven't done since Lir told me it was bad for my peripheral vision, choosing instead to tuck it behind my ears or pull it back.

Who needs peripheral vision, anyway?

19
The Day I First Met Lir

The day I first met Lir was also my first day of school.

I was already eight, three years past when I should have started. But learning things like arithmetic and how to properly fold a napkin had never been important to my mother. Nor was she big on birthdays. Every year on the day I was born, she would wake me with a small, unsalted oat cake that we would eat together, sitting on the front stoop while we watched the sunrise. Then she would give me a hug and a kiss, and we would go about our chores as if it were any other day.

She always said that age was just a number. That it was how we grew inside that mattered, and I could learn everything I needed to know from nature. How to know when it's time to harvest and plant from the color of the leaves. The importance of family and working together by watching an ant colony. What it means to love someone by observing a mother cat with her kittens, the way she nurtures them when they are little and defenseless then distances herself from them when they are old enough so that they can learn to care for themselves.

She taught me my letters and how to read and write, little scribbles in the margins of her grimoire next to the beautiful, hand-lettered spells and colorful illustrations she'd made herself. My favorite was one she never got to finish, the words a singsong rhyme that I played over and over again in my head in the days after she passed. *Blood and bone, heart and stone.* She showed me the best spots to dig for mussels in the sandy seabed. How to tell what kind of plant a seed will grow into just by touching it.

That wasn't good enough for the family service folk from the village, though. Two days after I turned eight, the captain of the police department showed up on our doorstep early in the morning.

Fergus Magee was young then too, the weight of his job not yet showing in his features, with bright orange hair that hadn't begun to thin and a bean pole frame. When my mother answered the door, he took off his hat respectfully and told her in an apologetic tone that he was there to take me to school. That it was nothing against her, but I had to get my learning with the other kids because it was the law.

I was hiding behind her skirts, frightened by the sight of a stranger. We rarely got visitors on the croft, and the ones who did come were always there to see my mother for a remedy for some ailment. So, I had little interaction with them, except to sometimes bring her an ingredient or two. I trusted my mother though, and when she told me to go with him, that we had to abide by the rules of the village folk, I obeyed.

My hand was tiny in his as he led me down the drive to where his car was parked.

I had never seen a car before, much less ridden in one. My stomach was a bundle of nerves while he started the engine. I clutched the sides of the too-wide faux leather seat the whole way into town, feeling every rut and crack in the road.

The schoolhouse was a long brick building built like the rest of County Kirk: practical. Meant to last against the abrasive sea air, not look particularly attractive. A few small shrubs poked their heads out of window boxes, and a flag flapped atop a tall metal pole out front. But that was all.

It didn't look at all like the kind of place that you

would send children to learn, and I wanted to cry. To beg the captain to take me home to the wide, open spaces and fresh air of the moor. I held it back as he walked me inside and handed me off to the principal, an older man in a tweed jacket that stretched against his ample belly. His mustache twitched when he talked. He asked me how old I was, and if I'd had any schooling before now. I told him I was eight, and that yes, sir, I could read and write as well as most people, I supposed. He printed my name on the top of a sheet of paper and then instructed me to go down the hall to the second door on the left. He was putting me in third grade.

I found the room easily enough. A lady with a nice smile and coiffed curls let me in. She introduced herself as the teacher, Miss McKinly, then led me to an empty seat and gave me a book and pencil. They were working, she said, on their spelling, and I could start at the beginning of the workbook until I was caught up, and if I had any questions to ask.

I nodded, too afraid to speak, and got busy. The words were easy enough to sound out, though there were lots I had never heard before. Like diagram and multiply. I could feel the eyes of my new classmates straying to me every time they thought the teacher wasn't looking, studying my homespun dress and simple shoes. When a girl wearing a pretty pink shirt in a desk close to mine pointed at me and whispered something to her friend that made them both giggle, I ducked my head, cheeks flaming, so they wouldn't see and concentrated on my work.

Lunch, at least, was something I recognized: milk in glass bottles that my mother and I had filled from our old, shaggy heifer, a slice of shepherd's pie with a flaky golden crust and fresh, crisp vegetables, and an apple fresh from our orchard. Though they served it to me on a red plastic

84

tray that felt foreign and flimsy.

The cafeteria was already full of kids eating and talking. Their laughter and the clink of forks and knives bounced off the walls. I did my best not to bump into anyone as I looked for a place to sit. I spotted the two girls from class nearby with their friends and was attempting to work up the courage to ask if I could join them.

They must have spotted me though because their faces scrunched up as if they smelled something bad. As if they could smell the poverty on me, although we had never gone hungry, and mum always made sure that our clothing was always clean and fit properly. Quickly, they scooted their chairs closer together, so there was no more room for me to squeeze in.

Tears pricked my eyes for the second time that day, threatening to spill over my cheeks. My throat was tight with embarrassment, and I was about to turn and run out of the room and eat my lunch in the loo when a soft hand touched me on the wrist.

"Don't mind them."

At first, I thought I was seeing double. Two boys with identical features, dark hair, and eyes like a freshly grown crocus flower sat alone at a table. They grabbed me, those eyes, like the wise, steady gaze of the long-legged gray heron that made its nest on the marsh. Then I realized they were dressed differently. Twins.

The one who'd spoken, who was slightly taller than the other, jerked his chin toward the girl's table. "Alice and Nerdane are nothing but *bhfostú suas* lassies."

I blinked. *Bhfostú suas.* Two more unfamiliar words. "What—?" My voice cracked, dry from not being used all day. I swallowed and tried again. "What does that mean?"

"It means stuck up." He grinned at me, eyebrows

lifting several inches as if he found my lack of knowledge endearing rather than insulting. "You're the girl from the croft, aren't you? Healer Ide's daughter. Clare Sage?"

I nodded.

He leaned forward, eyes dancing. "Is it true that you and your mum are witches?"

I bit my lip uneasily, but I saw no point in denying it. It would only make the rumors worse, not better. "Yes."

I expected him to look at me with disgust like the girls had. Or worse, run away in fear. Instead, he whistled appreciatively. "Wicked." He exchanged a glance with his brother, through which they seemed to come to some unspoken agreement, then turned back to me. "I'm Lir. This is my brother, D'arcy. You can sit with us if you promise not to hex us."

I slid into the seat next to him, trying to hide a smile. "I promise."

20
The Button

I am sweeping when I find the button.

It's hidden underneath my bed, in the farthest back corner, tucked between the wooden leg and the wall. When the bristles first brush against it, meeting resistance that shouldn't be there but is, I think it is another rock, or maybe a small ball of yarn that Nimbus was playing with before it got stuck, and try to maneuver it out. Only the harder I try, the more immovable it becomes, until I stand up, blowing out a frustrated breath, and it comes rolling out, as if pushed by an invisible hand.

The *clink-clink-rattle* it makes against the floorboards reminds me eerily of the sound of coins clanking together. Like the kind undertakers used to place over the eyes of the corpses they embalmed to help them buy passage to the netherworld long ago. I pause in my chore, one hand still wrapped around the broom, and bend down to pick it up.

It's been under the bed for some time, judging by the amount of dust and lint clinging to it. But when I wipe some of the grime off with my thumb, revealing the gold shine stamped with the initials LF, its identity is unmistakable.

An electric thrill, like being struck with lightning, shoots through me, making the hairs on my arms stand on end.

It was Lir's button, before it got lost. I can even remember the coat it must have fallen off, a dark green pea-style thing that hung just past his hips and hugged his shoulders exactly right and, with his dark features, always brought to mind the kind of deep, enchanted forest that witches like me were always said to live in inside story books. In fact, I realize, tightening my grip on my find, it was the exact same jacket Lir was wearing the night he left to go back to Galway. The night he disappeared.

A sudden gust of wind blows open the shutters, filling the cottage with an unearthly howl so loud it sounds like a lost soul keening to be found and scattering the pile of dust I had so neatly swept. Dropping the broom, I rush to close them. By the time I manage, I'm trembling all over, and I am no longer sure if I found the button by accident, or by design.

The only question is, whose design?

21
A Twin Thing

"So, what do you think, Clare?" Arleen gestures around with both hands.

I don't answer her right away. Afraid of how my voice might sound if I don't take a minute or two to get it under control.

It is almost the end of April. In two days, it will be Beltane and the day of my wedding. Yet rather than being excited, or even nervous, I feel as if a little bit more of me crumbles away with each minute that brings me closer and closer to the alter, as if I am made out of the same stone as the cliffs I am standing on.

What is worse, or better, perhaps, depending on which way you looked at it, is that no one else seems to notice. Not Cairn, who has come to call a few more times to meet my sister and begin moving his belongings into the cabin in preparation for our wedding night. Not Rush or Arleen who are so excited at the prospect of the upcoming nuptials that they probably wouldn't see a hand in front of their face unless it smacked them.

D'arcy has tried calling me several times since our last meeting, but I ignored them all. I know he wouldn't be fooled by my fake smiles and carefully constructed air of calm acceptance, and if he found out I was having second thoughts, he might try to talk me out of the marriage again, tell me that Cairn was dangerous, maybe even a killer, and that I ought to listen to my intuition. He is like Lir in that respect. They have both always been able to see through my lies. Maybe it's a twin thing.

Only I can't. I have too much to lose, have come too far down this road to turn back now.

Arleen is still talking, oblivious to the driving force behind my silence. Probably she has gotten used to my non-syllabic nature these past few days. She points to where the guests will sit, in the plain wooden chairs set atop the stand. Where Cairn and I will stand with the priest, under an archway closer to the surf. How we will go back to the house after the ceremony is over for food, drink, and music.

It sounds perfect. It looks perfect, a little girl's dream of a fairytale wedding come true. Yet I am barely paying attention, unable to get Lir out of my mind. I have tried. Brigid knows that I have. Only every time I seem to get close, something—a dream, a memory, a place, a smell—appears, catching me off guard, and it is like being run over by a freight train all over again, my muscles and bones and tendons all mushed together in one horrible, excruciating mess until the only thing I want is for the pain to end.

Like now.

The edge of the cliff is so close to my feet. It would only take one step, maybe two, to tumble over it and put a stop to my misery. My sister would probably even think it was an accident, tell everyone I slipped, lost my footing, and how tragic it was that it happened right before my wedding day.

"Clare?" My sister says my name again, bringing me back to the present with a lightning jolt, and I shake my head, discarding all thoughts of suicide. "I said, do you like it?"

"It's perfect," I reply automatically.

She beams, looking so satisfied that I feel a twinge

90

of guilt for being as removed from the planning as I have been. We should have been doing this together. Yet she has withstood the worst of it. "Good. I'm so glad."

"Clare!" Rush's voice calls from far off.

I turn, squinting, trying to see him. He is a small blur on the front stoop, waving at us.

"You have a visitor!"

I roll my eyes, making Arleen giggle. "Probably Cairn with more trunks. I swear, that man owns more clothes than any girl I've ever known." I link arms with her, and we make our way back to the house in step. Only when I come through the door, I stop short, blinking in surprise at the sight of D'arcy sitting at the table instead of my expected husband-to-be.

"Sorry to show up out of the blue, but I tried to call." He rises to his feet, looking not at all apologetic.

"I-I've been busy planning my wedding." The excuse sounds lame even to my ears. "I'm glad you're here, though. I have something I wanted to ask you."

I hear more than see my sister shoo Rush out of the house, closing the door behind them to give us the chance to talk alone. I really ought to thank her for how understanding she's been.

"What is it?"

"I'd like you to play the pipes at my wedding. I have already sent an invitation to your parents and Jack, but I don't think they'll be back in time to attend. It would mean a lot to me if you were there. And—" I gulp in air, tell myself to be courageous. "—I need you to go with me to Galway to get Lir's journals and put his flat up for sale."

I look down as I finish blurting out the words, too afraid to watch the reactions playing over his face. Instead, I stare at the floor, as if I looked at it hard enough and long enough, I could burn a hole in it with my gaze and fall

91

through it out of this world into the next.

Maybe Lir will still be alive in that one.

D'arcy places his hands on either side of my head and pushes my hair out of my face, tucking it behind my ears. The movement is so sudden, so unexpected, so much more familiar than we've ever been with each other, that I stand frozen for a moment, too shocked to react. Then I shake it back down, not liking how exposed I feel without it brushing against my cheeks.

"Stop doing that," D'arcy orders, though his touch is gentle when he shoves my hands away and tucks the loose strands back again.

"Why?"

"Because you're too beautiful to hide." His voice is a hushed murmur, so low that I never would have heard it if I hadn't been standing so close. It is exactly what Lir had said to me, the same day he'd told me about my peripheral vision. D'arcy had been there, standing half-forgotten in his brother's shadow like he often was when the three of us were together. I wonder if he remembers and if that is why he said it now.

This time, when I exhale, it is a little easier.

"So, will you?" I ask, changing the subject back to what we were discussing before.

"Yes." He lowers his hands to his sides.

"All of it?"

"All of it."

"Good." I pause, fiddling with the hem of my shirt. "I want to go tomorrow."

"I'm free. The captain gave me a little time off." His eyes cut to the side, not quite meeting mine anymore, and I know why without him having to tell me. His boss figured out he was digging into Lir's case again and told him to stay home, take some time to cool his heels until he

92

stopped.

"Okay. See you in the morning?"

"I'll pick you up."

I hesitate, wanting something more. To thank him, maybe. Or to break down and cry, knowing he will catch me and hold me until it is over. When I realize I am waiting for him to turn into Lir again, though, if only in my mind's eye, and stay that way, I stop and walk him to the door. He leaves, remaining himself the entire way down the road.

I never get what I want.

22
Myra

We take D'arcy's car to Lir's, a sleek, white thing with flashing lights on top and a cleverly hidden camera on the dashboard. We ride in silence.

The floor is littered with crumpled fast food wrappers and half-eaten donuts.

When we pull up outside the flat that my boyfriend called home, a tall, cold-looking mortar and brick building, we have to circle the round-about twice before we find a space to park. A brass plaque next to a call button outside the front door instructs us to press for entry. I do, and a moment later, a soft, feminine voice crackles through the speaker.

"Can I help you?"

"Um, yes. We're here for Lir Flynn's apartment? We have a key," I add as if this will make us more trustworthy. It must work, though, because, after a few seconds, the door buzzes open, and we make our way up a winding flight of stairs to the third floor.

A girl, the one who let us in, I assume, greets us at the top. She is fairer than me, her skin so pale it is almost translucent as if she is made of glass. A pretty doll, fragile and delicate, meant to sit on a shelf and look pretty. Not at all built for hard labor. Wide, light brown eyes blink out at us from behind oversized glasses.

"You must be Clare. Lir told me so much about you. And D'arcy, of course." She holds out her hands, grasping ours with her tiny fingers in greeting. "It's so nice to meet you both."

I share a surprised glance with D'arcy. "You knew

Lir?"

"Yes." She bobs her head, glasses slipping a little way down the bridge of her nose. She pushes them back into place with an index finger. "I'm Myra. Didn't he mention me?"

Her face falls at the blank looks on our faces, and she stumbles over her next words, trying to correct what is now an obvious mistake. "I-I'm sorry. I just assumed... Lir and I were in some of the same classes together at the university, I mean. Calc and-and fine arts. He was really smart. You look just like him," she adds almost wistfully, looking at D'arcy again.

"I get that a lot." His attempt at humor falls flat, and he continues quickly, obviously as eager to end this awkward conversation as she is. "Could you tell us which apartment was his? I think he mentioned it was one-twenty-six, but I'm not sure if I'm remembering correctly. It was so long ago, and I never had the time to visit."

"Of course." She waves for us to follow her, and we do, letting her lead us to a red wooden door. A glint on her finger catches my eye. A ring, an emerald on her left hand. A family heirloom, perhaps, or a gift from a beau. "It was actually number one-twenty-seven. You were close." She gives him an encouraging smile that he returns.

I push my way through them, irritated at the small talk, and insert the small skeleton key tied to a ribbon Lir had given me when he first moved in, in case I ever needed another place to stay, into the lock. I had never had a reason to use it until now. It turns easily, with a quiet click, and I open the door.

"Thanks for your help, but we can take it from here."

"You're welcome." She gives D'arcy a little wave as he goes inside, then lingers on the threshold, shuffling

95

from foot to foot, as if she wants to enter but isn't certain she should, or that she's welcome. I resist the urge to tell her she's not. That would be mean, and she looks like the slightest wind would blow her over. Front teeth worry at her lower lip, which I can see is already raw, slight frame lost in the baggy gray sweater hanging past her hips.

The jealousy that I have not felt since the night Arleen and I were in the kitchen rears its ugly head without warning. I see red, and green, the colors dancing across my vision like wildfire, and I realize with a kind of shock that I hate her, this girl I do not know. Not because of what she looks like or anything she's done, exactly. But for the time she stole from me with Lir, no matter how short it may have been. The severity of it is so strong, I have to blink a few times before it clears.

"Have a nice day." I dismiss her simply but kindly and go inside, leaving her standing in the hall. When I look back over my shoulder before closing the door, I see her vanishing back inside her apartment two doors down. I stare after her for another minute then turn to the task at hand.

There is a stack of mail on the small table in the foyer. I thumb through it, taking stock of the bills that will need to be paid and random junk—credit card offers, travel magazines—that can be discarded before stopping on one particularly thick envelope near the bottom. It is stamped with the familiar seal of the university, with a postage date of only a few days before Lir's disappearance. Curious, I use my thumbnail to open the envelope and pull out a stack of crisp cream papers.

The first is a letter from the dean confirming Lir's new full time student status. The rest are lists of housing options on campus, parking permits, and class recommendations. I read it twice, eyes darting over the

96

neat, professional script, sure there must be a mistake. Why would Lir have needed this? He'd been planning on moving back home after the spring semester ended like he always did. I would have known if he'd changed his mind.

I throw the letter in the trash, refusing to look at it one second longer, and wander into the kitchen. Here, a sink of dirty dishes waits to be washed, flies buzzing above the grime caked along their rims. I open the window to let them out, then search the drawers and cabinets for soap and a rag. Instead, I find only a jar of oats, a bag of sugar, and a half-eaten box of spongy cakes, the kind Lir hated because he said they tasted like cardboard.

What were they doing here, then?

Giving up on my search for something to clean the dishes with, I go to find D'arcy.

It doesn't take long. He's in what must have been the bedroom, judging by the frame and mattress pushed against the far wall. The air is dark and stuffy, with a stale air of unuse. I switch on the light, revealing tan walls where someone, presumably Lir, had stenciled a border of bookish quotes around the baseboard. The carpet is plush beneath my boots. A bookshelf full of script folders, notebooks, and various textbooks with broken spines stands in one corner, a chest so full of blankets that it couldn't completely shut in another. Lir's black typewriter, the old-fashioned kind with metal keys and ink ribbon, was half-buried beneath a mish-mash of loose pens, pencils, and papers, even a quill pen and a jar of ink, which littered the desk.

As if I know where I am going, drawn by some kind of womanly intuition, I cross to the desk. As I near, I notice there is a paper still in the typewriter. One of Lir's poems, I realize, as my eyes skim the words, but not one I recognize. A new one then. He must have been working on it before he went missing, and I read it again, slower.

97

My love has skin like burnished marble,
Her eyes a tiger's bronze.
Oh, that a road were in those eyes,
And I would travel it, no matter how long.
Her hair is a soft, downy pillow,
Her voice like that of a dove,
And I know no angel has ever sounded sweeter
When it sang out from above.

A stab of betrayal hits me deep in my gut. Lir's poems had always been about me. He'd said I was his muse. But this woman he described here didn't sound like me. My eyes were green, not brown, and my skin was freckled from the sun. Had he been writing poetry about someone else?

My mind turns to the girl in the hallway, her brown eyes and porcelain skin, then quickly dismisses it. Lir would never do something so dishonest. Would he? I remember the letter on the table, the snack food in the cabinet. I am starting to wonder if I had ever known Lir at all, or if I had only seen the person who I had wanted him to be.

Something dark and feather like brushes across the back of my mind, whispering in a voice that sounded like mine and yet nothing like me at all.

"You already know the answers to your questions."

Like a bird flying toward me down a pitch-black tunnel, it grows closer and closer, clearer and clearer, until, heart in my throat, I throw the curtain of my consciousness over it, too terrified to see what will reveal itself when it reaches the light.

Shaking my head to clear the cobwebs that have gathered, I open the small drawer cut into the front of the desk. Lir's leather journals are inside, right where I'd guessed they would be. D'arcy comes up behind me and

98

reaches around me to pick up the typewriter.

Balancing it carefully, he carries it over to the chair next to the window, where the natural light is best, and sits down. Lir loved that chair, despite its cracked leather seat and lopsided legs. It was one of the things he had insisted on bringing with him from home. He had told me once his best ideas for stories and scripts, even a few poems, had come to him while he was sitting in that chair.

D'arcy types a few keys. Nothing concrete, just experimental, yet the tears that have been waiting behind my eyelashes since I stepped through the front door burst free, silent rivers of grief. I sag against the wall, no longer able to hold myself upright, and a sob tears free from my throat. It was a mistake coming here. I should have paid someone to ship all of Lir's stuff to my house. At least then I could have mourned him in the comfort of my home rather than in this foreign, concrete jungle.

The typing stops. D'arcy has noticed my tears. "Clare? What's wrong?"

I force myself to look at him. My vision is blurry. "This room…that chair…the typewriter… He's everywhere and nowhere all at once. It-it's too much." My voice breaks on the last word, and I wrap my arms around myself, trying desperately to hold it together.

"Oh, I'm sorry." D'arcy sets down the metal contraption and stands awkwardly. "I only wanted to see if it still worked. I didn't think…"

"It's not your fault. It's mine. I can't stop thinking about him. I see him everywhere I go. When I sleep. When I'm awake. Everything reminds me of him, and I don't-I don't know what to do anymore. How am I supposed to live without him?"

I do lose it then, burying my face in my hands and tugging at my hair as I cry. My heartbeat is off-kilter. My

99

wails no longer sound like my own but like some mournful banshee grieving atop a castle parapet. My shoulders shake violently. My knees tremble, and I am about to sink to the floor in a puddle of my sorrow when D'arcy's hands close around my arms, sending shock waves through my body.

"Clare, that's enough. Calm down." He is using his cop voice, commanding me to stop, but I can't. If anything, I cry harder. He shakes me. "Clare!"

I shove him away from me as hard as I can, which given my current state wasn't very. He barely moves back two steps. I glare at him. "Don't tell me what to do." My voice rises to a manic shriek. "Stop telling me what to do! Lir is gone, and nothing you can say to me is going to change that, is going to make it better."

"Would you listen to yourself?" D'arcy's eyes widen at my combative tone. His voice rises to match mine as his agitation grows. "You're going to make yourself sick! Dead or alive, Lir wouldn't want you to be like this. He wouldn't want you mourning him so much that you can't even stand to listen to good advice!"

"Maybe so. Maybe not." My lips feel numb. "No one knows for sure what he would have wanted because he isn't here for us to ask him."

D'arcy moves closer to me, forcing me to tilt my head back to look into his eyes. For a second, I see Lir standing there instead, his gaze watery with tears. Then I blink, and it is D'arcy again, though his face and the tears in his eyes are the same.

"He would want you to be happy, Clare. I promise you that."

"How can you be so sure?" I ask, hating the pleading tone in my voice but unable to help it. I need to hear this, to have his blessing, at least, if I cannot have the one that I want.

100

D'arcy brushes a tear from my cheek. "Because he loved you."

His hand trembles where it touches me, and I can almost see him trying to convince himself to step back, to go wait for me in the foyer and drive me back home to get ready for my wedding tomorrow before he does something we will both regret. Only before he can, I kiss him.

I know he is D'arcy. In my head, I know that just as I know this is a mistake. But for a minute, I want to pretend that he is Lir again, that the man I loved so dearly is still alive and well and here, with me, and nothing has changed between us. I fully expect him to push me away, to stop me, to tell me that we can't do this. That it's wrong.

Except, he doesn't do any of that.

With a groan, D'arcy wraps his arms around my waist and pulls me to him, hard, returning my kiss with such intensity that my head spins. Is this how he has felt about me all along, and I was so blinded by my affection for Lir that I failed to see he was waiting for me to notice him? I do not know and am quickly lost in the movements of our bodies, unable to figure it out right now. His hands are all over me, pulling off my clothes and touching my bare skin. I do the same, more ravenous for the touch of flesh on flesh than I have been in a long time.

Somehow, he maneuvers us onto the bed. My hands grip his shoulders. My legs wrap around his waist, and he kisses me again, all sloppy lips and wet tongue, as he slides inside of me.

I arch my back, fingernails digging into his spine, marking him. Time seems to freeze as pure, unadulterated pleasure floods every nerve ending in my body. I can taste my heart in the back of my throat as he begins to move, in and out, in and out. When something warm and salty drips onto my lips, I realize I am crying again, and breathe his

101

name.

> At least, I think it is his name.
> It might be Lir's.

23
The Noise a Body Might Make

The drive back to Kirk is silent save for the purr of the car's engine. Lir's journals were safely stowed away in a box in the trunk, and I had called the real estate agent the Flynn's lawyer had recommended, putting the loft up for sale.

The salesperson on the other end of the phone had been excited at the prospect when I told him where it was and said he didn't think it would take long at all to secure a buyer. I was glad.

I wanted it gone, especially after what I'd done.

I chance a glance at D'arcy from the corner of my eye. His gaze is hard, glinting in the evening light coming through the windshield, his jaw like a straight line of steel. He drives with one hand on the wheel in a white-knuckled grip. I can tell from the set of his shoulders that he is mad. Although who he's angrier at, me or himself, I don't know.

Still, I want to say something. To apologize. To ask him whose name I called out. To demand to know why he hadn't stopped me when I kissed him. To let him yell at me, hit me, call me a whore, tell me that we may as well have spit on his brother's grave and that he hated me.

I say nothing, though, too scared, too much of a coward to face the truth.

He doesn't either.

We park at a truck stop diner halfway home that advertises "all-you-can-eat rashers" and go inside. He gets us a seat at one of the red plastic tables with two menus, and I head to the bathroom in the back.

After doing my business, I splash icy water onto my

103

face and stare at my dripping reflection in the dingy mirror. In the harsh light of the fluorescents, my skin looks pallid, my eyes shallow. My lips are swollen from D'arcy's kisses, the bottom one cut from where he bit me a little too hard.

It hurts when I touch it with my tongue. Yet I relish the pain. I deserve worse.

I grab a handful of paper towels from the dispenser to dry my face when a shadow moves in the corner of the room behind me. I haven't heard anyone else come in, and look over my shoulder, expecting to see another traveler heading for one of the toilets. Instead, I face an empty wall.

A second later, the pattering of feet reaches my ears, followed by the sound of a stall door slamming. I jump. The damp wad of towels falls out of my hand, and I grip the sink for purchase. My fingers are clammy.

"Hello?" I wait, straining to hear a reply, the sound of someone breathing, something. But there is nothing. I try again. "Who's in here?"

Still, no reply comes, though I wait almost a full minute. The only sound is the *drip-drip* of water coming from the faucet and the pounding of my heart. When I have managed to convince myself I imagined the whole thing, a scuttling sound, not unlike the noise a body might make as it squeezes into a corner, comes from the stall I left.

I am gripping the sink so hard now that I am surprised my fingers don't leave indentations in the tile. Forcing myself to move, though every bone in my body screams at me to run in the other direction, I creep across the room toward where the person, or whatever it is, disappeared. As I get closer, I see no shadow on the floor, no shoes sticking out, no indication that anyone is in there. The lock isn't turned in the door, and it opens easily when I push it.

"Hello?"

104

The stall is empty, toilet paper untouched and the lid of the commode closed. The light flickers overhead as I step inside, casting eerie shadows across the walls. I peer into every nook and cranny, though there is nowhere for anyone or anything to hide. I even look in the other stalls, despite having heard no more movement. Only when I am satisfied that I was truly alone do I wash my hands and leave.

The only explanation I have for what I heard is that my guilt mixed with my grief has finally become too much for me to handle, and it caused me to hallucinate another being in the bathroom who was never there.

D'arcy has ordered for us by the time I return, sliding into the booth across from him. Two plates of sausages with toast and jam, and two glasses of orange juice. The sausages are overdone and greasy, the jam too sticky, the juice too sweet. I manage to eat only a few bites then wait for him to finish and pay the waiter before we head back to the car.

We have only been driving for a short while after leaving the diner when he speaks. "We need to talk."

"I know." And I do.

He blows out a breath, shoulders relaxing as if he thought I was going to fight him, and is relieved I didn't. "What we did was wrong."

"I know," I repeat, my voice small.

He looks at me then. "You still love him, don't you? My brother." There is no point in denying it, so I don't try. "I know it wasn't me you were thinking about back there. It was Lir."

I wince at the accusation in his tone. If he feels for me the way I now suspect he always secretly has, I can only imagine how my actions have hurt him.

His expression softens. "Look, I don't care why you

105

kissed me, Clare. And call me crazy, but I don't regret what happened between us afterward, either. I think a part of me has always…" He chokes back the admission neither of us wants to admit, affirming my suspicions. *Loved you.* "Cared for you. I wanted to be there for you, and I was. But that still doesn't make it right. Lir was my brother. He was your best friend, your fiancé. He loved you, Clare. He loved both of us. What we did dishonored his memory. Not to mention that, convenience or not, you're engaged to be married tomorrow."

My heart leaps, my eyes widening in fear. "Oh my gosh. Cairn. What if he finds out? He'll be furious at the slight, and his father might use this against me, use it to null the wedding and take the croft. I'll lose everything! I…"

"He won't find out. I won't breathe a word of what happened today, I promise, on one condition."

I peer over at him, fearful of what he is going to say next. "What kind of condition?"

"That you swear to me that you didn't feel anything back there, not a single ounce of affection for me. That you were thinking only of my brother, and that you still prefer a marriage of convenience over one of love." He takes one hand off the wheel and places it atop mine. "I don't have a lot to offer you, Clare. A detective's life isn't glamorous, or safe by any means. I know this isn't exactly the best timing, but I've spent my whole life holding my tongue, letting other people go first, get what I want, and I can't do that now, not when there's even the slightest chance there might be something between us. So, if you will have me, I promise, you will still get to keep your family's land, and I will do my best to be a good husband."

I stare at his hand covering mine for a long, long time until I can see the first spires of the houses in the village up ahead. It is a good offer, as good as any I have lately, yet still not the one I want.

Slowly, to let him down as gently as I can, I pull my fingers free of his. "I can't. I'm sorry."

"Why not?"

I tell him the truth. He deserves that much, after everything else. "Because every time I look at you, I only see your brother. And no matter how hard you try, you will never be him."

He nods, and turns back to the road, though I can tell by the rapid bob of his throat that I have wounded him deeply. "Then I wish you all the happiness you deserve and will be at the ceremony to play the pipes as you asked."

107

24
An Omen

"Here's to the bride-to-be!"

"Cheers!"

My sister and her boyfriend, a sweet-tempered boy with cherub cheeks and brown hair that tumbled onto the frames of his round, silver glasses who'd shaken my hand with nervous, sweaty fingers when he arrived earlier today, clink their glasses together and down their single malt. I do the same, feeling the amber liquid burn as it runs down my throat. No bridesmaids.

It is only hours before my wedding. I had barely changed out of my travel clothes from Lir's house when Arleen whisked me back out the door for my bachelorette party, telling Rush to keep an eye on the property. Now, I sit in a smokey pub as a bartender with a full-faced beard brings us another round of shots, our fifth. I down mine without waiting for the others. They are laughing, gabbing above the music coming from the band on stage, not paying any attention to my less than celebratory behavior. I hadn't asked for a party. It seems silly, given the circumstances surrounding my upcoming nuptials. But as usual, Arleen had taken matters into her own hands and planned one anyway.

Oh, well. At least I get free booze.

I down another shot and look around as I let the liquid settle in my stomach, where it sits like the flame in a lantern, glowing and warm. The pub we have gone to is large, almost quadruple the size of my house, with a wooden dance floor covered in bobbing, weaving people who look like they are having the time of their life.

I wish I was one of them.

The bartender brings another round, and we drink them together. Arleen puts her arms around me and gives me an uncoordinated hug. Her words are slurred.

"I love you, big sis. Congratulations!"

"Thanks," I reply with what I hope is a convincing smile, pushing her away from me gently so that we don't topple off our stools. She laughs and reaches for another shot. I do the same, then freeze with my hand around the glass.

Someone is standing across the room, his back against the wall. Someone whose hair falls forward into his eyes, a smoldering look on his face. Someone who looks like…

"Lir," I breathe.

"What?" Arleen looks at me in confusion, not having understood me thanks to all the noise.

I don't answer her as I slide off my stool and shove my way through the crowd. People tell me to watch where I am going, to butt out, get a grip. But I ignore them all, not even caring when I stumble and almost fall several times thanks to the liquor coursing through my system. I reach the other side of the room and look around.

He is gone.

I hear a door close behind me and spin.

It is the door to the parking lot.

Past caring about how foolish this is, only that I get some answers, damn it, I square my shoulders, shove open the door, and go outside.

The parking lot is dark despite the lampposts spaced around the edge. Shuffling footsteps come from my right, and I turn around in time to see a shadowy figure disappear between two parked cars. I sprint after him, sliding on a patch of loose gravel and nearly falling flat on my face.

Somehow, I manage to catch myself and grab him by the arm.

"Lir!"

"Hey!" The figure, not Lir at all but a dark-haired guy half his height, shoves me off. "Let go of me, lass! What are you, off your kilter?"

"No, I thought—" I gasp for air that refuses to come. My lungs feel like an invisible fist is crushing them. Or maybe that is my heart. Who knew disappointment was so heavy? I should have known better than to get drunk with the way I'd been seeing things lately. "I thought you were someone else."

"Yeah? Well, my condolences to him." The guy shakes his head and gets into his car, muttering under his head about crazy women and the trouble they cause.

"Sorry," I call after him, lifting my hands and then letting them fall back to my sides with a sigh. He pulls away, tires squealing, and I turn to go back inside. As I do, a shadow passes overhead, and I look up, expecting to see a moth fluttering around one of the streetlamps. Instead, a crow perches on top of the closest light post. Its wings are an ebony black in the dark, and it cocks its head, fixing me with a beady-eyed stare.

A cold hand trails down the nape of my neck.

If it were any other bird, maybe I would put it off as a mere coincidence. But everyone who still practices the old ways knows what our ancestors did: that crows are the harbingers of the Morrigan, the goddess of death, Brigid's dark opposite. And seeing one is an omen that she will visit you soon, in one form or another.

The old wives' rhyme my mother used to recite when I was a girl and the birds would roost in our field, hunting for field mice and stray seeds plays through my mind.

110

One for sorrow, Two for joy,
Three for a girl, Four for a boy,
Five for silver, Six for gold,
Seven for a story yet to be told.

I stare at my lone visitor, waiting for it to fly away, too petrified to move. When it doesn't, I inch backward until I am out of reach of its sharp talons, then run inside, slamming the door behind me.

25
A Case of Chicken Pox

The girls at school had always been cruel. Witch girl, they called me. Moor child. Croft trash. They would hold their noses when I walked by to turn in my tests as if the smell of manure lingered on my skin. Laughed at my homespun dresses as if they were a joke compared to their modern, name-brand garments.

Lir protected me from the brunt of the teasing, always walking me to and from class. Sitting with me every lunch. Yelling at them when their taunts became too sharp. And they would listen.

He was cute, and his family came from old money that had lived in Kirk as long as mine. They wanted him to like them, to pay them attention and pretty compliments. Unfortunately for them, he saw them for what they were—empty, vapid things as ugly on the inside as the underside of a clam. He had eyes only for me, and they hated me for it.

I could see it in the way their gazes would narrow and sharpen sometimes at Lir and me across the room when they thought I wasn't looking, and in how their lips pressed together in disapproval, then turned down as they scratched a hasty note and passed it to their friends.

Still, they didn't dare confront me directly, not with Lir around. But he couldn't follow me everywhere.

They finally managed to corner me one day in the bathroom. I was wearing a new dress, a blue and white gingham that my mother had spent weeks sewing, my hair tied back in two long braids. They cornered me in a stall, pushed me down and ripped my dress, then held my head in the toilet bowl until I thought for sure I would drown. One of them had a pair of scissors and used them to cut off my braids then threw them into my lap. They left me sitting in a puddle of water and tears, my hair an ugly, uneven bob.

I ran home without telling anyone where I was going, where I fell into my mother's surprised arms and sobbed until my emotions were wrung out to dry. She patted my head and told me not to worry. Hair always grew back, and those girls would get their comeuppance. We would see to that.

The next day, I returned to school wearing a straw bonnet, and several small dolls woven from corn silk in my pocket. The girls laughed at my headwear, as I had known they would, but I ignored them. Kept my chin high.

When they weren't looking, I stole bits of hair from the brushes poking out of their bags and spent the rest of the class gluing the different colored locks to the doll's heads underneath my desk. That night, my mother and I buried them beneath the oak tree in the backyard beneath the light of the full moon with a handful of chili peppers. As she filled in the earth over each of their featureless faces, I whispered the names of each girl three times.

The next day, first Alice, then Nerdane, and the rest of their friends started itching uncontrollably in the middle of class and had to be sent home. A case of chicken pox, the teacher said.

They didn't come back for two weeks. When they did, I slipped them a note, saying that if they ever hurt me again, I would do a lot worse to them than give them a temporary illness.

They left me alone after that.

26
A Lost Soul

On the morning of my marriage, Arleen wakes me up before the sun with a cup of clover tea and a plate of corned beef and cabbage. She waits until I have finished eating, then fills the round metal tub with warm water and scrubs my skin with a pumice stone until it is pink and shiny. She braids flowers and spells into my hair, helps me get into my dress, and adorns my bare feet with silver knots and crosses.

When I am ready, she leads me over to the mirror, so that I can see how beautiful I look. I have to agree she is right. My hair is a halo of fiery curls around my face, and a bridal flush colors my cheeks. Yet my eyes reveal the cavernous sorrow aching in my chest, threatening to crumble at the slightest breath, and I cannot banish the feeling that this, somehow, is the beginning of the end rather than a new beginning.

The wedding is a simple ceremony down on the beach, with only our families and a few close friends in attendance. My sister walks me down the aisle. Neither of us had any idea how to get in touch with our father. He's missed so much of our lives that it seemed pointless to invite him to such a significant event as this one.

D'arcy plays the uilleann pipes, the low, mournful wail marking the pace of our footsteps. I look up at him once, and his face shifts and changes until it is Lir standing there, his long dark hair pulled back into a smooth ponytail, his eyes boring into mine, a sure, confident smile on his lips as they close around the blow stick. Teasing me. Mocking me.

I almost stop, confess what I've done right there in front of everyone. Then my hand is in Cairn's. He pulls me to stand beside him beneath the wooden arch decorated in greenery. And I don't.

The priest binds our hands together with ribbons and recites the ancient marriage rites over us. One at a time, we drink the chalice he holds to our lips, then slip the rings onto each other's fingers. Mine is a cold, heavy thing made of iron, yet oddly attractive in its simplicity. I wonder if Cairn had it made especially for me, or if he picked it out of a case filled with dozens of other similar ones. When he leans forward to kiss me, to seal the bargain, I press my lips chastely to his and close my eyes. A rush of heat shoots through me, so unexpected it makes me gasp, and my heart flutters against my rib cage as if trying to escape.

Cairn feels it too, judging by the warmth in his eyes as he pulls away, and I take a quick step back before he can try for more. We return to the house, arm in arm, and greet our well-wishers as husband and wife.

Later, after the wine has been drunk, the fruitcake has been eaten, the broom has been jumped, and the last guest has left, I sneak out to the barn, leaving Rush and Cairn to do the dishes, and lead Rhiannon into the yard. I don't even bother saddling her, but instead mount her bare back. I am still in my wedding gown, yet I don't care. The need to move, to breathe, to put as much distance between myself and Cairn as possible until I forget about the press of his lips against mine, is stronger than any sense of propriety or decorum.

I kick her in the sides, harder than I normally would, and we take off at a gallop, riding pell-mell across the moor. The farther we go, the faster I push her, letting the fresh air clear my mind. When lightning splits the sky, followed closely by a peal of thunder brought on by my tumultuous mood, and the clouds split open, drenching us with rain, I know this is dangerous. It is too dark for me to properly see where we are going, and one stray rock is all it will take for a horseshoe to slip, or worse, a bog to claim us both. Yet I don't turn back, even when the mud comes up to Rhiannon's ankles and she slows to a quick trot to keep her footing.

A large black bird flies out of the trees next to us, cawing loud enough to wake the dead. Rhiannon rears, whinnying, and I scream, nearly toppling from my seat. One powerful hoof connects with the bird's chest with a sickening *crack*, knocking it out of the air. Gripping the reins with all my might, I jerk them until I get her back under control. I dismount, panting, and press my face to her quivering side.

"Easy, girl. Easy. It's all right. You're all right."

I repeat the words, keeping my voice low until the whites of her eyes stop rolling and she calms. I straighten, and grab for the reins again, intending to lead her back home. I don't know how many miles we've gone, and the thought of slogging back through the wet grass is unappealing. As if in response, the rain lifts, and I send a quick thank you to the heavens.

Caw!

The crow we hit, or at least I thought we did, flies out of nowhere and lands on a nearby stone jutting out of the ground. I shriek, dropping the reins, and Rhiannon takes off in the direction of home. I shout for her to stop, even chase her a few feet, but it is no use. Blowing out a frustrated breath, I turn to face the bird, hands on my hips, prepared to give it a good scolding.

Recognition pools, thick and viscous, in my lungs.

116

I know it is impossible. After all, there are probably hundreds of crows that all look the same in these parts. Yet this one watches me as if it knows me too. I am sure now we did hit it, and it somehow survived. This is the same bird I saw at the club.

With another shrill cry, the crow spreads its wings and flies back into the scrub forest. I can't see where it is going, but I can hear the swoosh of its wings through the air, and I follow it, holding my dress to my knees to keep from tripping, ducking under low-hanging limbs and stepping over high-rising tree roots as I struggle to keep up. Right when I think I've lost it, I see its eyes glowing at me in a small moonlit clearing beyond the tree line, and I step out of the brush, relief making me weak.

It is short-lived.

The crow is not alone. With him is a whole murder of black-feathered birds, some sitting on the ground with their companion while others watch us from the trees, as well as a figure dressed in black. Dirt mats his clothes, his skin, his hair. When he steps into the light, I fall to my knees, shock and disbelief stealing my ability to stand.

"Lir?" I whisper his name, too afraid to speak it aloud lest he evaporates into thin air like the apparition he most certainly is. Only D'arcy isn't here this time, and the longer he lasts, the more I realize that this isn't something my mind has made up.

He shuffles toward me, and I see that he isn't as solid as I first thought. The few leaves that litter the ground crunch under his feet. Yet his face swims in and out of focus as if it was too difficult for him to maintain for long, and where the moonlight hits his body, I can see through it to the trees behind him, as if peering through a thin curtain.

He is a *thevshi*, a lost soul doomed to wander the world forever after death, unable to find its way into the

117

beyond. My mother always talked of them like some sort of boogeyman, meant to keep children inside after dark but not real. Now that I am face-to-face with one, I know I ought to be afraid, that I should run from this place and never look back or think about what I've seen. Only I am not. I do not. I drink in the sight of him, unable to look away. He looks the same as he did the day he'd left to go back to Galway. He is even wearing the same clothes.

There are differences, I realize. His gait is uneven, one leg moving stiffer than the other, so that it drags behind him, leaving streaks in the dirt. His shirt is torn and ragged. Dried blood crusts the hair on the back of his head, and one of his eyes is a milky, unseeing white. His lips are twisted in a grimace as if he is in constant pain.

The thought is a knife to my heart.

He kneels on the ground in front of me, a haunted look in his gaze.

"Lir, it's you. It's really you. But how? How are you here? I don't understand. You look... Are you...?" I whisper the words, reach for him—to draw him to me, to comfort him—but he puts a finger to my lips, shaking his head. His skin is cold. His fingernails smell like earth and rot. Revulsion swims in my gut, but I ignore it.

With his other hand, he picks up a stick lying nearby, and I tense. Maybe he is a vengeful *thevshi*, mindlessly killing any humans who crossed his path. Or maybe he isn't Lir, but an evil wood sprite who has taken on his form to trick me into trusting it only to lead me to my death. Instead of striking me, he lowers the wooden tip to the ground and begins to write something in the dirt.

Dead.

I knew it. In a way, a part of me had always known. I just hadn't wanted to admit it because admitting it would make it true. No one who stayed missing that long came

118

back alive. Now, staring at the word, I can no longer deny it.

"How?" I ask, though again, I think I already know the answer. The abandoned car on the side of the road, with all of his things still in it. The suspicious lack of evidence. The wound on his head. How his body looked like it had been buried.

He etches another word in the earth, the stick making little *scritch-scritch* sounds as it moves back and forth.

Murder.

All of the breath leaves my lungs in a violent whoosh as I rock back on his heels, staring at his ruined body. His dead body, I think. The body that someone killed, stole the life from, from me. Guilt steals into my veins, followed closely by confusion. After all, it's not my fault that he was killed...is it? Anger washes the question away almost immediately, entwining with my sorrow and making me grind my teeth.

"Who did this to you?"

The crow cries out, its voice piercing the night like the midnight chime of a clock. Lir looks up, his movements sluggish and startled. It hops onto his shoulder, and pecks at his hair as if trying to tell him something. Whatever it is, he seems to understand it, because he reaches out and grasps my hands, his expression suddenly urgent.

"C-Cl-Clare." He forces open lips sealed shut by mud and moss, and he hisses my name on a breath that smells of decay and wet wood. "You...please...help me."

"How?" I beg, squeezing his fingers as tightly as I dare. I fear I will hurt him more than he already is.

"Free me, and I-I can p-pass on."

"Free you from where?"

"Where I was-was trapped. Am still trapped. I came

119

here to-to tell you again, but I do-don't have l-long."

"It was you." Understanding washes over me as I recall the crow in the parking lot, how sure I had been that I'd seen him at the pub, the mysterious shadow in the loo after D'arcy and I left his house. "At the diner and the pub."

"Yes. In your dreams t-too. I've been-been trying to-to reach you, but it-it's hard to g-get through."

"Shh. It's okay." I press my forehead to his and close my eyes. "You don't have to explain. You're here with me now. That's all that matters."

He gives a hitching sigh. "I can-can't stay. I wish things had-had been different. I'm sorry for ev-everything. But you must face the-the truth. Only then can I b-be at peace."

Something tickles at the back of my mind, some piece of information that my gut tells me I ought to know. Instinctively, I recognize its importance, and try to pull it to the forefront of my memory. Yet every time I reach for it, it slips further away into the gray recesses of my brain, until I question whether it was ever really there or just one more figment of my tortured imagination. After all, what could I possibly know about Lir's death that would help him move on?

The crow takes flight without warning, soaring out of the trees with another caw, and Lir dissipates as if made of smoke.

I grab for him, trying to catch him, to make him stay, but get only air. "Lir!" I leap to my feet and spin around, searching the shadows for any sign of him. "Lir, wait. Come back. You have to tell me what you mean. Please, come back!"

There is no answer, though. No sign of him, or the bird that led me to him, save for a single black feather that

120

floats down onto the ground at my feet and the steady chirp of cicadas coming from the trees.

27
Only One Course of Action

Lir is dead.

Of that, I am certain.

After all, hadn't I seen his ghost?

Just as I am certain that his death was not an accident like the police led us to believe in the end, but the result of human malice.

A human malice that he had come to me for help unmasking.

And with every step I take back out of the trees and across the moor toward home, I become more convinced that I have only one course of action from here: to uncover the identity of Lir's murderer and make them pay.

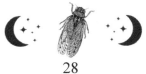

28
The Rattle of a Chain

"D'arcy!"

I beat on the door of his house hard enough to rattle the wood in its frame. I came here right after leaving the moor, had hooked poor Rhiannon to the cart, and driven it so fast it was a miracle I had not thrown a wheel. The moon hung low above the tree line. Only a few hours of night left before the sun came up. Somewhere in the distance, a wolf howled.

"D'arcy, open up. It's me!"

I am about to give up—maybe he hadn't come home after the ceremony but instead gone into town to drown his sorrows in the bottom of a bottle—when I hear the rattle of a chain as the security lock unbolts. A second later, the door swings open, and D'arcy peers out at me, bleary-eyed from sleep and the bottle clutched in his hand.

Looks like I was right about the drowning sorrows.

"Clare? What are you doing here?" He is wearing nothing but a long shirt and looks me up and down, taking in the mud on my slippers, the tears in my dress, and bedraggled hair. "What happened to you? Where's Cairn?" He looks past me as if expecting to see my new husband standing on the porch behind me.

"At home. I'm sorry. I know I shouldn't be here, but I didn't know where else to go."

I push past him into the house before he can stop me. He closes the door, and I spin to face him, unable to hold back the words any longer.

123

"I saw him, D'arcy. I really saw him!"

"What are you talking about? Saw who?"

"Lir."

"What?" He drops the bottle onto the carpet with a thud and grabs me by the arms, his eyes widening so far, I worry they will pop out of their sockets. "You mean he's alive? Where is he?"

"No."

"No? How did you see him, then?"

"I saw his ghost."

Disbelief swims across D'arcy's features, and I hasten to explain.

"Look, I know how it sounds, trust me. But it's true. I swear. I saw him before too, but I thought I was imagining things. Seeing what I wanted to see, you know? Only tonight..." I gulp for the air to continue. "After the wedding, I went for a ride. A bird, a crow, startled Rhiannon. She almost threw me, and I wound up alone on the moor. That's where I saw Lir."

"Clare..."

"He came to me, D'arcy! He told me he was murdered, and that he couldn't pass on until the person behind his death was revealed. Don't you see?" I stare up at him, begging him to understand. "This is why I haven't been able to move on since Lir disappeared, because he still needs me. I have to help him! I have to find out who the killer is."

D'arcy drops my arms, looking sad. Wrinkles that I am sure hadn't been there before his twin's death pull at the corners of his mouth and eyes. Death ages us, in many ways.

"Look, Clare, you've been through a lot lately, all right? Lir going missing, his case being closed, the memorial, what happened at his flat, the wedding, your

124

horse getting spooked. It would affect anybody. You don't have to fabricate stories to make yourself feel better. No one is going to judge you for grieving, not even now that you're married."

"I'm not making this up. I really saw him, D'arcy!"

"Stop!" He slams his palm down on the table, making both me and the lamp jump. "Just stop it, all right? I wish you had seen my brother. I would give anything to know that he's okay, wherever he is. But what you say happened? It's not possible, Clare."

"Possible or not, I know what I saw. Lir's not okay, D'arcy. His spirit is trapped on this plane, unable to move on. If we don't do something, he'll be stuck that way forever!"

"Fine!" D'arcy throws up his hands, making frenetic shadow puppets on the wall. "Let's pretend I believe you, and you saw Lir's ghost. What are we supposed to do about it?"

"I told you. We find the person who killed him."

"And then? We what, turn them over to the police? Get justice for his death? With what kind of proof? I doubt they're going to come with a signed confession that says *I killed Lir Flynn.*"

"No." I glare at his scathing tone. "Lir doesn't need justice. It's too late for that. He needs everyone to know the truth, about how he died, where he died, and who put him there. Once I identify who the murderer is, I'll follow them until they reveal where they hid Lir's body. Then, you can lead the police there, and I can make them pay."

"Make them pay," he repeats, eyes narrowing. "You mean…" He lifts a hand abruptly and shakes his head as if he doesn't want to hear another word of what I'm suggesting. That I will take vengeance on Lir's killer. "No. This is nuts, Clare. It's too dangerous. You can't."

125

"Yes, I…"

"Clare, I'm serious. Listen to me." D'arcy puts his hands on my shoulders much gentler than before. "It's late. Go home. You'll feel much better in the morning after you've had some sleep. We can talk about this again then, okay?"

"I don't need sleep, D'arcy." I shrug off his touch, frustrated at the way he is talking to me, as if I am some injured animal that has to be soothed. "I need to save Lir. And if you're not going to help me…"

"Help you? You're talking about killing someone, Clare!" He hisses the words, gaze darting toward the window as if worried someone will overhear us.

"Someone who killed your brother."

"It doesn't matter! It's still taking a life. Even if you did somehow manage to find the person who murdered Lir and they didn't kill you first, do you think you could do the same to someone else?"

"I…" I hesitate, remembering how Lir had looked in the clearing. A rotting corpse. D'arcy was right. It was fine to talk about seeking revenge, but doing it? That was another thing entirely. Was I capable of dooming someone to that kind of fate? "I don't know. But I can't let them get away with what they did, either."

"And they won't. If you're right, and Lir was killed, it's only a matter of time before someone finds his body and reports it to the police. Then, I promise you, I won't rest until the guilty party pays for what they did."

"No one is going to find his body." I'm not sure how I know that, but I do. It is a feeling in my gut, one that settles beneath my intestines like warm cement, most likely based on how unfruitful the investigation into his disappearance had been. "If they were, they would have done so by now. It's up to me to find the truth."

126

"Fine." D'arcy sighs as if finally realizing this is one argument that he isn't going to win no matter how hard he tries. "Just promise me you won't do anything rash, okay? You won't go looking for the murderer, or Lir's remains, without checking in with me first. If by some magical force, you're right about all this, then there's a killer out there who thinks they got away with murder. Snooping around in their business could be dangerous."

It is an easy enough request. A smart one, even. The kind an inspector with years on the force would make. Yet the way he watches me as he waits for my answer, with an eerie intensity in his eyes that wasn't there before, makes me feel uneasy.

For the first time, several pieces of the puzzle I have been working on since Lir's case was closed fit together with an almost audible snap. D'arcy's feelings for me, harbored in secret our entire lives and now come to light only after Lir was gone. His jealousy toward his brother, which he outright admitted at the funeral. How he had failed to solve his disappearance, and the way he had been so quick to accuse Cairn and his father of harming Lir to get to me.

A cold, sick dread pools in the pit of my stomach. It is impossible. Unthinkable. D'arcy couldn't have killed his own brother, then used the investigation to cover it up. He wouldn't have, would he? And I... Had I slept with my boyfriend's murderer?

The thought is too reprehensible to imagine, and I try to banish it as quickly as it came. Yet now that the idea has been given a voice, it refuses to be silenced, and I am suddenly, achingly aware of how late it is, how alone we are, and how no one knows where I am, save for the man in front of me.

Part of me wants to demand the truth, right here and

now. But how can I? How can I look him in the eye and ask if he had killed his twin so he would have a chance at a life with me without Lir getting in the way? Especially when I have little evidence at best. The other part is terrified that D'arcy will see the questions dancing behind my eyes, and of what he might do should he recognize my suspicions for what they are.

Needing to put some space between us, I open the door and step out onto the safety of the porch. The night breeze stirs my loosely bound hair around my face, tickling my cheeks like spider webs.

"I promise."

29

The Damage is Done

Naked sheep run to the other side of the pasture, cool and happy, as I drape the freshly cut wool over the fence and begin to beat out all the dirt and mites. With every hit, I release a little more of my frustration.

Whack!

D'arcy's body pressed against mine.

Whack!

How Cairn kissed me on our wedding day.

Whack!

The look in his eyes that said he wanted more, but only if I was willing to give it.

Whack!

The sight of Lir's ghost on the moor.

Whack!

The word he wrote in the dirt: murder.

Whack!

My irritatingly brief list of suspects.

Whack!

Was it D'arcy, who had feelings for me that went deeper than he ever would have admitted when his brother was alive? Who had been the lead detective on the case since day one, yet somehow wasn't able to turn up a single worthwhile clue despite his track record for always getting his man? Who had tried to dissuade me from tracking down his brother's killer and tried to deflect suspicion, first onto Rush, then on Cairn?

Whack!

Was it Rush, my loyal companion of the past seven years? He had been out of work for months when I hired him, thanks to Lir. Had his desperation for a job, a steady wage, a roof over his head, and food in his belly, mixed with a need for revenge driven him to do the unspeakable? Had he eliminated Lir, thereby removing the competition, putting a balm on his wounded pride, and creating an opening that forced me to take on help to stay afloat all at the same time?

Whack!

Or had D'arcy been right, and it was Cairn? Had he and his father wanted my land so badly that they were willing to resort to killing and extortion to get it?

I straighten, stretch my aching back, and look across the way to where my husband stands in the upper field, helping Rush pick the last of the apples. The first of the rabbits have come out of hiding in the heather, hopping around as they nibble the purple blooms and digging fresh burrows among the tall stems. I see them every morning when I go to pull the weeds that would choke the delicate roots if left to grow too long. White cotton tails and twitchy pink noses.

I don't see Brigid though, not yet. Perhaps, like me, she is running late this year. Or maybe she is choosing to stay hidden, kept underground by the dog that follows Cairn out of the sea mist lingering around the trees each day, some new fowl or rodent that his master shot down clutched in his jaws. A prize that he proudly delivers to me so that I can clean it and cook it for our dinner. Never a rabbit, though. Cairn has stayed true to his word and kept his dog out of the fields.

Still, maybe she senses some danger in the beast, some wild instinct that cannot be tamed, and stays away.

Cairn hasn't tried anything since that moment at the

altar, either, or brought it up, for which I am grateful. The doubt swirling inside me over whether or not he played any part in Lir's death renders it impossible to reconcile any affection I may have otherwise felt toward him, making me jumpy every time we are around each other, spooked at the thought that I might be sharing my home with a cold-blooded killer.

He must have noticed, because he has kept his distance. We even made a second bed and put its headboard back-to-back against mine so that we could sleep separately. He is the perfect gentleman, rising before I do and going about his chores without complaint so that I can take breakfast and a bath in solitude before getting started on my day's work. More than a pretty face, it seems. It is unlikely that he would go to so much trouble to earn my trust if he had something nefarious going on.

Then again, I think, watching him laugh at something Rush says, dropping another apple into the barrel. Perhaps it is all part of a dastardly plot. Maybe he intends to win me over, and once my guard is down, kill me too, making him and his father the sole owners of the croft the way Lord O'Brian wanted it all along.

A shadow passes over me, momentarily blotting out the sun, and I shiver, rubbing my arms to get rid of the gooseflesh. I start to gather the wool, now ready for the dyeing barrels. Yet when a cry splits the air, I spin back around.

A crow has swooped down over the field, undoubtedly having made its nest in the tree they are picking from and is attacking Cairn for disturbing its young. He bats at it, yelling wordlessly, as it tangles his hair in its powerful black wings. I can't be sure from this distance, but I have the instinctual feeling that this bird is the same one as before. Lir's crow, as I have come to think

131

of it.

Cairn teeters, the ladder wobbling beneath him, and I grab my throat, holding back a gasp. He is going to fall. He hits the ground hard, the ladder crashing onto its side, and I cannot tell if he is okay. Immediately, the crow is on him again, furious at the invasion.

I am running now, one hand holding the hat protecting my face from the worst of the sun, yelling as Rush chases the crow off with his pitchfork. When I draw close, I see that he is still breathing. The bird squawks at us from a higher branch, out of Rush's reach, and I draw up short, exhaling in relief. Though whether for my husband or the bird, I am not sure. Still, the damage is already done. Bright red scratches line one side of Cairn's face where the bird's claws got him, dripping into his eyes.

I take him inside, where I clean the cuts with warm water and goldenrod, then apply a salve of chamomile to help speed the healing. We are so close that I can smell the blood, iron and bitter, feel the heat of the day rising off his skin as it cools. My fingers tingle nervously where they touch him, the fine curve of his cheekbone and the sharp plane of his jaw, uncomfortable at our proximity when we have spent every moment since our wedding night dancing around one another.

When I tape a patch of gauze over his temple to protect against infection, he winces.

"Sorry." I say it automatically, though I am not sure what I am apologizing for. That I hurt him? If he killed Lir, I would do far worse than press on his wound too hard, and the timing of the crow's attack seems too serendipitous to ignore, as if it were trying to send a message.

Beware, there is a threat here.

"It's fine. My pride is hurt more than anything else." He smiles up at me, and he looks so sheepish that I can't help but return the gesture.

It is the sunny change in my disposition that does it. Makes his eyes turn into liquid pools as if he is just now realizing how close we are to one another. He reaches for me, slowly, giving me time to run. When I don't, too frozen in place to move, he places his hands gently on my hips, drawing me between his legs.

Our gazes remain locked as I lift trembling fingers and run them through his hair. It is as soft as I imagined. Is this a trick, I wonder, meant to convince me to let my guard down around him so he can stick a knife in my back when I least expect it? Or is this real, a second chance at love, and was the crow warning me against Rush, and Cairn merely happened to be in the way?

He lifts his chin, lips slightly parted, and I decide there is only one way to find out. I lean down to kiss him, to claim his mouth with mine and drink in the taste of him until I am sated.

A loud yowl, followed by a series of barks, splits the silence, and we pull apart as Nimbus dashes through the open door. Mastodon, who has been trained to stay outside, stops on the stoop and whines, droopy eyes fixed on his prey. I wish he had gotten rid of him before he moved in but knew better than to ask. Dogs are bad luck on a croft, scaring away the fairy spirits that come to bless the crops. Satisfied that she is safe, Nimbus hops onto the bed and begins grooming her tail.

Cairn is still holding onto me, though his grip has gone slack. I step away from him, suddenly uncomfortable, the moment broken.

He blows out a frustrated breath. "Do you think those two will ever be friends?"

I look between the animals and shake my head. "I wouldn't count on it. The expression fighting like cats and

133

dogs is popular for a reason."
    He says nothing in reply.

30
A Boy

A nature witch's work is never truly done, a fact that I am reminded of when Alani Magee-Connolly shows up on my doorstep the next morning.

I have just finished washing the breakfast dishes when her knock sounds on the doorframe, timid and feminine, and I go to greet her, drying my hands on my apron. Her eyes are mistrusting, the pale green irises speckled with red, a sure sign that her stomach is bothering her. Still, she dips her chin, and a moment later I know why when she tells me the reason she has come.

She is carrying her first child and wishes to know if it is going to be a boy or a girl. Her mother, she said, used to tell her tales about my family's prowess in midwifery, before she passed. She can pay good coin and offers me a small sack of coppers. I weigh it in my hand, not bothering to count it in front of her, before placing it in the pocket of my apron.

"Very well." I lead her over to a chair at the table and have her prop her feet up on the table. Crossing to the jewelry box on the shelf, I rummage through the contents until I locate what I need: my mother's silver wedding band strung on a matching chain. The words *love is magic* are carved into the inside.

I used to believe that was true. Only, like my mother, I suppose I too learned the hard way that it wasn't.

I touch the promise ring Lir gave me, the one which now sits on my right hand instead of my left, remembering again with aching clarity the last time I saw him. How I had walked him to his car, helped him load up his luggage, then...what?

My forehead wrinkles, nose scrunching. For the first time, I cannot recall what had happened after that. Surely, I had hugged him, kissed him goodbye, told him I loved him then waved until his car disappeared over the rise like I always did before going inside and getting ready for bed. But it was as if someone had taken a cloth and erased that part of my memory, leaving only a blank slate in its place.

The thought made my pulse speed a little faster, my breath come a little shallower. I peer out the window, where Rush and Cairn are busy hauling fresh hay bales into the barn. Was there something my mind had forced me to forget, something so horrible it was trying to protect me from it?

No.

I wave the idea away like one would a cobweb. I am being overly paranoid. I am tired, that's all. I haven't been sleeping well since the night of my wedding. A few days' rest, some warm food and plenty of liquids, and I will be as good as new.

For now, I have a job to do.

I carry the charm over to where Alani waits and hold it over her belly, which has started to show. I close my eyes and concentrate on what I want to know, projecting the question out into the universe.

What will the sex of this baby be?

When I open my eyes, the chain is swinging back and forth from east to west.

I wind it up around my fist and look at my latest customer. "It will be a boy."

She sits up straight, feet dropping to the floor. Her ankles, I observe, are slightly swollen beneath her socks. "You're sure?"

"Positive."

"Thank you." She gets to her feet, looking from me to the bulge in my apron. "I can bring you more if that isn't enough."

"It's plenty," I assure her, then go to the cupboard and fill a small jar with dried dandelion and nettle leaves. I press it into her hand, waving away her protests. "For the water retention." I gesture to her legs. "Take one teaspoon with your breakfast each morning."

"Thank you." She squeezes my hands before I can pull them away. Her eyes are clearer, brighter than they were before, and I realize the mistrust I'd thought I saw earlier had been worry over what my answer might be. A boy meant that her husband's name would be carried on for another generation. Happiness glows from her pores, her joy infectious, and I pull my hand roughly away before I can catch it.

I had always thought I would have a daughter someday the way my mother had, and her mother before her, and my grandmother before that. Someone to pass our family's lineage down to. Someone to continue Bridget's work. And, I suppose, thinking of Cairn and his golden hair and easy smile, I still could. Except, the only child I ever wanted was with Lir. Now that he is gone, it seems wrong to share that experience with someone else.

I nod, the only reply I trust myself to give, and she leaves me standing alone in the empty kitchen, suds drying beneath my fingernails, hurrying home to tell her husband the good news.

137

31
All-Encompassing Darkness

When my father left, I swore that I would never trust another man again.

Even at my youthful age, I understood what it meant when he went away and didn't return, and no news of his death reached us. He didn't want us anymore. We weren't good enough.

For the first couple of months after his departure, I made every deal I could think of with the deities when I said my *paidirs* each night before bed. That if they brought him back, gave our family a second chance at love, that I would be better. Kinder. Neater. Prettier. Smarter. That I would work harder and speak slower. Listen more. Smile bigger, and cry less. Whatever it took to be the perfect daughter that I had obviously failed at the first time. But either my wishes were ignored, or they chose not to grant them, because they never came true, and little by little, I hardened my heart against others, until even my mother and sister had a tough time breaking past the walls I had so meticulously built.

Lir changed all that.

Like a mason with well-skilled hands and tools, he took down every stone I had erected to shield myself from the outside world and the pains it contained. Piece by piece, he chipped away at my defenses, with a soft word here, a kind gesture there, until nothing stood between us. Even now, I'm not entirely sure how he did it, and whether it was really through any effort of his at all. Perhaps I'd secretly been waiting for someone to come along and notice me, and when he did, I unlocked the door and threw away the key myself, giving him an effortless way in.

Being with him was its own kind of unique freedom. One where I was a completely different person than the simple peasant girl everyone else saw. In his eyes, I was beautiful. I was a queen, intelligent and strong. I was enough to make him stay, or so it seemed before death so rudely intruded upon our lives. And every time I started to shy away, too afraid of getting in too deep lest I drown, he always said and did exactly the right thing to draw me back in again.

He was the hunter, and I was his prey, and I went into every snare he set for me willingly, even though it meant being the object of his affection was its own kind of prison. After a while, everything I did, everything I said or was or became in his presence revolved around him. Soon, I was no one without him. Even when we weren't together physically, I could still feel him there, a tether knotted in the middle of my soul, pulling me into his orbit, and I loved every minute of it in the same way an addict loves a drink.

Until that chord was cut without warning, and I was left floating in the ether, suspended neither here nor there, lost in the kind of all-encompassing darkness that it was impossible to escape.

32

What Madness Looks Like

Is this what madness looks like?

I stare at the cluster of random objects laid out on the table in front of me—the bloodstained rock from the drive, the crow feather, the button from Lir's jacket, the picture I'd found crumpled up in his room—trying and failing to make sense of them. There is no doubt in my mind at this point that Lir's ghost is leaving them for me, which means there is a purpose behind his actions. These baubles are clues meant to help me put together the missing pieces of what happened the night he went missing and solve the puzzle of his death.

My fingertips delicately trace the blood splatter on the rock that had long since stained its earthen surface in a macabrely beautiful pattern. There is something I am missing. I am certain of it. Some message he is trying to convey through each one of these items that I cannot quite make out. Like the night I saw him in the trees, it buzzes in the back of my mind like a cicada's wings, fluttering just out of my reach. Only every time I try to grab hold of it and pull it closer to examine it, it dances away as if made of smoke. Almost as if I know the answers I so desperately seek, yet for some reason cannot recall them.

With a sudden rush of irritation, I snatch up the objects by the fistful and throw them into my jewelry box before slamming the lid. Closing my eyes, I take a deep breath through my nose and run my hands through my hair. I am getting nowhere like this. I have no idea how to do what Lir's spirit has asked me to do, am no closer to solving the mystery of his murder than I had been the day I got the phone call that his parents had given up the search. And if I fail, he will be doomed to wander the world for the rest of eternity, unable to pass on, yet unable to be fully here, either. As hopelessly lost as I am.

I can no longer pretend that this is a game, or something made up only in my mind to comfort myself in his absence. Lir needs me, needs my help, has transcended the laws of death and the afterlife to communicate with me at what I can only imagine is a great and painful effort on his part. I have to stop chasing ghostly doubts and do what I have been putting off: start questioning my suspects. It is the only way to get real answers, to fill in the gaps left behind by the objects' silence, and finally put both my soul and Lir's to rest.

33
The Truth of Words

My opportunity to question Rush comes a few days later when the three of us are repairing the fence at the end of the pasture. It is hot, laborious work, and Cairn has gone inside to get some of the lavender lemonade I mixed up last night. His stallion runs through the field nearby, tossing its mane and kicking up its hooves, happy to not be cooped up for a change.

Rush glances up at it as it passes, a smile on his face. "Good to see him enjoying himself. It's a shame, how Master Cairn keeps such a beast locked up. An animal like that ought to be free."

"I suppose so." I watch him from the corner of my eye, careful to keep my head down so that he won't notice, as I lift a new board into place. It feels strange to suspect him, almost a betrayal of the relationship we have built working side by side all these years. He is as much a brother to me as if we shared the same blood, and I am reminded of the time when I accused Arleen of taking my favorite doll, only to find it at the back of my closet a week later. She refused to talk to me for a week afterward. "Kind of like Lir, don't you think?"

He frowns, either annoyed when the hammer strikes the nail crossways, bending it or by my change of subject. "What do you mean?"

"Oh, nothing. I've been thinking. What if he's still trapped somewhere that the police can't find? That would be horrible."

"Aye." He wedges out the useless nail and hammers in another. This one goes in neatly. "Although, I wager he'd be dead by now if he were."

"You're probably right," I mutter, trying not to let him see how much his words get to me. "Still, if someone were to find his body now. That would be pretty bad for the person who put him there. Don't you think?"

"No more than they would deserve," Rush grunts, swinging the hammer a final time.

I jump, picture it coming down on my skull, crushing the delicate bone. Was that what he'd hit Lir with? I peer at the handle as much as I can without being obvious when he passes it to me, biting my tongue and forcing a smile to keep from gasping when our fingers touch. Is that blood on the tip or rust? I can't be sure. Sweat trickles down my shoulder blades. I slip it into my pocket when he isn't looking, then kick the toolbox closed before he can notice. D'arcy will be able to test it. Then we'll know for sure.

I feign thirst and hurry back to the house as quickly as I can without rousing his suspicions, leaving him to put his things away. However, my relief at being away from one suspect is short-lived when I find myself confronted by another as soon as I come through the door. Cairn leans against the counter, taking a long drink of lemonade. I chew on my lip, debating slipping back out to hide the hammer in the garden instead, then decide to ignore him. Going to the sink, I busy myself with washing my hands.

Undaunted, he comes up behind me and presses his cup to my neck. The icy cool of the glass is a balm against the sun-blistered back of my neck, and I lean into it with a groan against my better judgement.

"Feel good?" he murmurs, voice inches from my ear.

"Very." I turn toward him and let his free hand cup the side of my face, searching his eyes for some sign that he killed Lir to gain ownership of my land. But all I see in them is longing, deep and strong, and when he dips his head to kiss me, I think only that this is how I will fall. Only at the last moment, he stops, his lips a hairsbreadth away from mine. His breath is warm and sweet, like him. Or at least, the him he shows to everyone.

"You still miss him, don't you?"

I nod, forehead brushing his. I don't have to ask to know if he is talking about Lir. "I do. I think a part of me always will."

"I understand. And I will never ask you to forget him. Still, I hope you come to think of me fondly as well. Do you think that's possible?"

I study his features, wishing I could read him better. But he is nobility, trained in the art of deception, and his face is a closed book. "I might. If your father hadn't been after my family's land for years and just so happened to propose our union right after Lir's case was closed."

He stares at me for a long moment, then laughs abruptly, throwing his head back. The sound prickles against my flesh, making my hair stand on end as I recall the crow in the field, how it'd attacked him, pecking at his head and driving him away from Rush and me. Was this what it was trying to tell me, then? Or was it trying to warn him away from the real killer?

"Is that what you think? That my father kidnapped Lir and held him in the basement so that you would have no choice but to marry me?"

When he says it that way, it sounds derisible. The fantasies of a silly girl seeing ghosts where there are only shadows. Still, I stand my ground. I have come too far to back down now. "You have to admit, the timing was more

144

than a little convenient. I would be a fool not to wonder whether he helped it along to get what he wanted."

He shakes his head as if disappointed in me. The idea stings more than I like. "Allow me to waylay your suspicions, then. My da may be a greedy old curmudgeon who's not afraid to seize a good opportunity when he sees one, but he didn't get to where he is today by getting his hands dirty. Trust me."

I wait until he is gone, eyes following the line of his body as he heads back out to the field to help Rush, taking the rest of the lemonade with him, then pull the stolen hammer out of my pocket. I wrap it in brown paper and twine, then scribble a hasty note to D'arcy about my suspicions and what I need him to do with it. I put the letter into an envelope addressed to him, slide it under the twine, then drop the package into the mailbox, where it will be picked up in the morning.

145

34

An Expert in Poisons

I go to bed fully clothed that night and lie awake staring at the ceiling until Cairn returns from the field. Then, I shut my eyes and pretend to be sleeping. I hear him pause by the bed, staring down at me, before shedding his work clothes and splashing water onto his face and under his arms. There is a creak as he crawls onto the mattress, followed almost instantly by the sound of his snores. When I am sure the valerian root I'd hidden under his pillow has done its job and he will not wake, I slip out from beneath the blankets.

On bare feet, I creep to the cupboard, where I pull out the thick, leather book that belonged to my mother from its dusty corner. I blow it off, revealing the designs etched into the cowhide. A five-pointed star. A single, staring eye. A twisted, leafy branch. A jar of honey surrounded by bees. A crow, its talons extended and wings outspread. And a Dara knot.

The spine groans as I open it, and I flip through the pages to the hollowed-out section inside, where glass bottles in all shapes and sizes rest in wood compartments. Each one has a small piece of faded white tape stretched over the front, where the name of the ingredients inside has been scrawled in small black letters. Ide Sage was a diligent herbalist and an expert in poisons.

I select the ones I want—snakeskin, hellebore, gypsum weed, and grave dirt—and set to work grinding each one in the stone mortar and pestle. These powders I put in the small black cauldron over the fire, then add a ladle full of water and a drop of dragon's blood that hisses when it hits the surface. I bring the mixture to a boil, then quickly remove it from the fireplace and spoon it into an empty bottle, then cork it to keep it from spilling.

When I hold it to the light, I can see the power of the poison I have made swimming through the clear sides of the vile. One sip of this, and whoever killed Lir will die a quick and painful death, their insides boiling.

I don't know why I think I can solve Lir's murder when the police were never even able to find proof that he was dead. Or why it's so important I do. People disappear all the time. I know that. Living in a remote village on the edge of a moor that borders a steep drop-off to the ocean below comes with numerous dangers, which have claimed more than one life over the years.

A hidden bog that looks like solid ground until you step on it and you are sucked into murky oblivion. Wild animals not picky about where they get their meat. Fairy stones that have the power to transport a person into the realm of the fae queen if they are foolish enough to step through them.

But it feels different this time because it's Lir, someone I loved and knew. The tortuous ball of emotions inside my chest demands I reveal what happened to him. And I can't help but feel that the girl we'd met in Galway, Myra, knew more about it than she was saying.

I remember the way she had lingered outside Lir's flat as if she wanted to go inside but was afraid to. Either because of what she might find, or who was in there. I need to know what she knows, no matter how small or insignificant it may be.

Thankfully, Lir's journals are full of homemade bookmarks keeping his places, including a napkin with the name of a bar and a phone number written on it in marker. There is a lipstick mark on one corner of the paper cloth as if someone had used it to blot their makeup. The pale pink is the same shade as Myra's lips. I stare at it for a minute, a small nerve ticking at the corner of my eye. Then, I dial the number and ask to speak to her.

The man who answers, her manager, I guess, says she's working, but that she can call me on her break in a couple of hours, and would I like to leave a message?

I hang up without answering, grab my bag, ride Rhiannon to the station, and buy a ticket to Galway. At the last minute, I remember my promise to D'arcy and, despite my misgivings, call him from a payphone to let him know where I am going in case something happens to me. He's not at home. The machine picks up on the fifth ring. I leave a quick message before hanging up and hurrying to catch my train.

35
The Floral Rose

Galway at night is a buzzing beehive compared to the sleepy city it was when D'arcy and I visited during the day. The sidewalks are packed, the buildings lit neon. College students stand in every doorway, drinks in their hands and laughter on their lips. It's not hard to find the tavern where Myra works. The first person I ask points the way to a small, brown brick building wedged between a butcher shop and a theater.

The atmosphere is quieter here than the one outside. Soft lights greet me when I push through the door. The air smells of tea and beer. A small stage with a red velvet curtain acting as a backdrop sits along the far wall. A girl dressed all in black sits on a single stool, reading a poem into a microphone to the small but attentive crowd.

I find a booth in the back corner easily and slide in, scanning the room for Myra. I find her quickly, wielding two bottles of pale ale and stout behind the bar like a wild west cowgirl. When she's finished making the drink, I wave her over, and she comes, wiping her hands on a damp dish towel. As she nears the table where I sit, her eyes light up in recognition.

"Hey! It's you. Clare, right? What are you doing here?"

"Just taking in the nightlife and thought I would stop in for a drink. What's good here?" I pretend to scan the bottles lined up on the shelf behind the bar. I have no intention of imbibing on anything tonight. But maybe if I buy something, she'll be more inclined to talk than if I requested information for free.

"I like a cuppa of the floral rose. I'm not a big drinker."

"I'll take one of those. Make it two, and you can sit with me for a minute."

"Well, we're not supposed to drink on the job." She chews her lower lip, eyeing the man with the beefy arms behind the MC stand. This must be her boss. "Still, I am due for a break in a few minutes. So, what the heck. Why not?"

She retreats through the swinging doors to the kitchen, then returns a few minutes later with two mugs balanced on saucers. She sits one in front of me and keeps the other for herself as she takes the seat across the table. The smells of ginger and cardamom are redolent, and I take a swipe of the whipped cream on top with my finger.

She stirs hers with a small spoon, letting it cool. "I'm kind of glad you came back. It's been so hard since Lir disappeared, not being able to talk to anyone about him. No one at uni knew him as well as I did."

I don't miss the meaning behind her words, and envy flutters its wings again, followed by suspicion. How well did she know him? I try to force a smile, but it tastes sour. "I would imagine not. He wasn't exactly the social type. In fact, it's odd that he would have befriended you so quickly. Did the two of you spend a lot of time together?"

She must miss the venom in my tone, because she echoes my smile with one of her own. "A fair amount, but Lir was much more comfortable with a book than he was with people. That's how we met, you know. In a study group for our fine arts class. As soon as he quoted Shakespeare to me, I knew he was someone worth getting to know."

150

"Really?" I feign casual interest as I prop my elbows on the table. Now we were getting somewhere. "A study group? Who else was in it?"

"Just a few other guys from the class. I don't remember their names." She shrugs. "We never hung out after that."

"So then, there was no one else at school Lir was friends with? No one he spent time with outside of class while he was here?"

"Not really, no." She shakes her head, then purses her lips, thinking. "Well, except his brother when he came to visit. Although, I hadn't seen him for a few weeks right before Lir disappeared. I thought it was weird, because they'd had a fight the last time he was here, and I never knew if they made up for not. Then, the next thing I know, Lir's picture is in the newspaper and his brother is leading the investigation searching for him."

"Lir and D'arcy had a fight?" My heart skips a beat. "About what?"

"I—" She breaks off suddenly as if realizing she's said something she shouldn't have. "I don't know. I could hear them through the walls, shouting at each other, but I couldn't make out everything they were saying. Something about how D'arcy didn't approve of what Lir was doing, and Lir telling him to mind his own business. That he had it under control."

"Had what under control?"

"I don't know." She picks up her tea, not meeting my eyes. "So, you and Lir. You were close, right?"

I force myself to stay in my chair when what I want to do is reach across the table, grab her by the collar, and shake her until she tells me everything. "Yeah. We've been friends since we were kids and dated since high school. We were even planning to get married right before he went

151

missing."

She chokes on the drink, splashing it all over the table and her lap. Alarmed, I reach over and pat her on the back as she coughs, trying to catch her breath.

"Are you okay?"

"I-I'm fine. Sorry. It just-just went down the wrong pipe." She wipes the mess with a handful of napkins, then gets to her feet, collecting the dishes. "I should get back to work."

"Wait!" I grab her wrist, tighter than I mean to. I loosen my grip, trying to act normal when it feels like my chest is going to explode. "You acted surprised just now. Was it something I said?" An idea, horrible and ugly, like a worm hidden at the center of an apple, pops into my mind. "Did Lir not tell you we were engaged or something? Why wouldn't he bring that up, unless the two of you were...?"

"Look, I wish I could tell you more, but I really need to go before Eddie notices I'm over here. It was nice talking to you."

She hurries away as if she can't escape my questions fast enough, vanishing into the kitchen. A few minutes later, I watch as she emerges again, in a fresh shirt and apron, carrying a bag of rubbish. Using her free hand, she pushes open the emergency exit and carries the trash outside.

After only a brief hesitation, I follow her.

36
Is Someone There?

I am standing in an alley. I can hear the muffled stop and go of cars on the street a few feet away. The tavern and the buildings beside it tower over me like giants lurking in the night, waiting to swallow me whole. What little light streams from their windowed eye sockets is dimmed by the moonless sky. Yet, I can make out the shape of a cluster of small trash cans and one large dumpster against the far wall.

Myra is nowhere in sight.

The dumpster's lid is half open, unable to close due to an object hanging over its rim. Curious, I creep closer, wanting to see what it was. With both hands, I lift the lid a few inches, startling a cat that has been feasting on refuse inside.

With a screech, the stray bolts from the dumpster, scaring me so badly that I cry out and fall backward over the smaller cans. The lids roll, spilling trash everywhere. Panting, I watch as the beast vanishes around the corner then wait until my heartbeat returns to normal before getting to my feet.

Something squishy coats the back of my pants where I'd landed, and I scraped my elbow in the fall. Grimacing at the smell and the pain, I open the dumpster slower this time, keeping a wary eye peeled for any other critters that might be enjoying a late-night snack, and pull out the offending object.

Immediately, I drop it with a scream, staggering

153

back. The arm—the human arm—hits the side of the dumpster and tumbles to the ground. A ring with a ring stone sparkles dully on its left forefinger. My heels connect with something solid, and I go down again, pinwheeling my arms. Panting, I push myself up, turn to see what it is I tripped over, and recoil in horror.

It is Myra, or what is left of her. One arm is missing, blood dripping from the stump of her shoulder. More of the red liquid dribbles out of the gaping hole in her chest, where the hilt of a blade juts out. I half fall, half crawl to her side. Blood stains my palms and the front of my skirt, yet I barely notice. Grasping the hilt, I yank it out with a sickening squelch, hoping she will revive. But her eyes stare up at me without blinking, wide and unseeing.

The sound of something jostling the fallen trash cans makes me jump. I drop the knife with a clatter as I scramble to my feet, and spin around, my heart beating wildly in my throat. "Hello? Is someone there? Who is it?"

No reply comes from the shadows. I feel the unmistakable prickle of hair on the back of my neck and have the uncanny sensation that I am being watched. Panic and instinct take over, and I stumble over the scattered litter, fumbling along the wall for the door, feeling for the knob. I think I am screaming for help, though my ears are ringing so loudly I can't be sure it's not in my mind. My fingers have closed around it when something hard and heavy, like a trash can lid, hits me from behind, and the world is all stars. The last thing I see is a gold pocket watch swinging in front of my face, a thistle etched into its front, then darkness.

37
A Believable Story

I wake up in bed, the quilt pulled to my chin and a cold rag pressed to my forehead. Cain and Rush sit next to me, their faces lined with strain and worry as if they have been there a long time.

Rush notices me stir first and claps my husband on the leg. "Cairn. She's awake!"

Cairn is out of his chair in an instant, leaning over me. The concern in his eyes is startling. "Clare! Thank the stars. Are you all right?"

"I-I think so." I remove the damp cloth and push myself up, wincing as a burst of pain shoots through the back of my skull. My fingers find the goose egg hidden beneath my hair. "What happened?"

"D'arcy brought you home. He said he found you in an alley in Galway. That there had been another murder. You've been unconscious for hours. We thought you weren't going to wake up."

"D'arcy?" I struggle to remember. But fireworks are going off in my head, popping behind my eyelids and making it hard to concentrate. I gesture toward the cupboard. "Bring me the feverfew."

Rush hurries to do as I ask, and I place a pinch of the dried herb on my tongue and let it dissolve. Immediately, I feel better. More clear-headed.

"What were you doing there?"

"I went to meet a classmate of Lir's," I tell them. I see no point in lying, not now. "I thought she might be able to tell me who would have wanted Lir to disappear. Only someone killed her before I was able to convince her to talk to me."

I glance toward the laundry bin, where the tip of my blood-soaked clothes peeks out. Myra's blood.

"You said D'arcy brought me home?"

Dim flashes come back to me now, of familiar footsteps running toward me through the alley. A voice shouts my name. The pocket watch dangles from his pocket. Sirens scream in my ear. D'arcy's arms lift me out of the car, carrying me inside.

"He said you called him," Cairn explains, "left him a message telling him where you were going. He went after you as soon as he heard it, but by the time he got there, it was too late."

It's a believable story. Plausible, even, except for one thing. The other presence I had sensed in the alley after I found Myra. How D'arcy hadn't been home when I called despite being temporarily laid off. His insistence that I tell him before investigating Lir's death. The way he had kissed me, hungry and desperate, and the fight Myra had said he and Lir had right before he went missing that he never told me about. Never told anyone about. I couldn't help but wonder, had D'arcy been there all along?

Had he followed me to the tavern and killed Myra before she could reveal any more of his secrets, then knocked me out so he could swoop in and play the savior? Or had there been someone else in the alley with me, some dark, unseen entity who had murdered, first Lir, then Myra, and now would be coming after me next? I look around, but the cabin is empty save for the three of us.

"Where is he?"

"He had to go back to the scene to make an official statement. I expect an officer will come by in a few days to

156

take yours as well. He said he would return to check on you as soon as he was able."

When he does, I think, feeling for the small vial in my pocket, where the poison rests, safe and ready to administer, I will be ready to get some answers of my own and, if necessary, act.

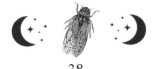

38

The Monster in the Mirror

The doctor Cairn brought to treat me prescribes a tonic that looks like congealed syrup for my head wound. I refuse to take it, trusting instead in my own herbal remedies and a combination of bed rest and gentle exercise wherein I take short laps around the house. It is during one of these, as I shuffle stockinged feet over the floor like a cautious babe taking its first steps, that something moves out of the corner of my eye.

I am alone. The men are out in the barn, shoeing the horse. The animals are asleep on the porch. My thoughts go immediately to Lir, that he has come to visit me again, and I spin toward the figure, so quickly it makes me dizzy.

It takes me a minute to realize that I am looking at my reflection. Cairn, at some point, I am not sure when, presumably while I slept, must have removed the sheet from the looking glass over the dresser. I had not even noticed until now. I was so used to it being covered. I study the girl staring back at me as if seeing an old friend who has become a stranger, and for a minute, it is just me, Clare Sage. The same as always.

Then, I start to notice the differences.

This reflection is dark. Shadows that are not present in the sun-filled room cling to its edges. The hair is the wrong color, black instead of red. The clothes are different, a black dress with a full skirt that would be more at home spinning around a ballroom floor than working on a croft. The face is the only thing similar, but where I am not smiling, this reflection smiles at me so widely that I can see all of its teeth, wide enough that I can imagine the sound of its cheekbones cracking. Slowly, so slowly it seems to move in time with the pounding of my heart, it raises an object in its hand, and I realize with a cold, bone-drenching horror that it is the bloody knife used to kill Myra.

I know enough about the spirits who dwell on the other side of the mirror world to know what to do. Seven years of bad luck be damned. I smash my fist into the glass, breaking the mirror to keep it from coming at me. In the glass shards that litter the floor, I see with no small amount of relief my reflection is normal once more. Yet the feeling of skin-creeping dread in my chest does not dissipate.

My mother always said that people, like magic, had two sides: a light one and a dark one. It was up to us to decide which one we would be. Secretly, I had always wondered if it was really that easy. Black and white. No gray areas. Or if there were times when the darker part of a person took over because it needed to, in order to protect its lighter half and do what it could not.

Does this make them a monster?

What is a monster, really? A woman who kills her abusive husband to save her life and is forced to serve five-to-ten in prison because he was technically unarmed at the time? Or the man who beat her bloody and bruised for years? A person who looks different, dresses different, speaks different, has a different skin tone or practices a different belief who is ostracized, condemned, and burned at the stake for it? Or their executioner?

Humankind fears what it does not understand, what it cannot control, because we recognize the propensity for good and evil within every human soul. So, we label these things as wicked, as taboo, and say our prayers in hope that the light will be enough to keep away the ever encroaching

160

dark. Yet try as I might, I could not shake the thought that I had just seen my darker half, and that she was more alive and well within me than I had heretofore thought possible.

39
The Moor Witch Arrested for Murder

It is the police captain, Fergus Magee, who comes to the house two days later.

He looks different from when he'd come to take me to school—his belly is bigger, sagging over his belt, and his hairline has begun to recede, forming a widow's peak. But he holds his hat to his chest the same way and asks respectfully if I wouldn't mind coming down to the station with him to answer a few questions regarding the murder of Miss Myra Thorpe.

Cairn is there, putting together some cold-cut sandwiches for his and Russ's lunch. When he hears the request, he joins me in the doorway and asks the captain why I need to go downtown. Haven't I been through enough? Surely anything he has to ask me he can ask here.

Fergus wrings the brim of his hat as if he can draw water from it. He wishes he could, he says. But the boys in the city are all over this one, claiming jurisdiction because of where she'd been killed. Turns out, my fingerprints were the only ones found on the knife that had been used to kill Myra. In their eyes, well, that made me a suspect, and he'd been given strict orders to bring me in for questioning.

I protest. My fingerprints were only on the knife because I'd pulled it out of her. I had tried to save her, not kill her.

The captain bobs his head and says of course. He understands that, but orders are orders. If it looks like he is showing favoritism toward me, it will only make things worse for both of us. He'd appreciate it if I would kindly come with him of my own free will without making a fuss so he wouldn't have to handcuff me.

Time seems to slow to a crawl as I make my way across the yard. There is a muffled roaring in my ears as if my head is underwater. I hear Rush's muffled exclamation of surprise as he comes around the side of the house and sees what is happening. I ignore it and don't look his way.

I keep my chin up as I slide into the backseat of the police car, tucking my dress neatly around my ankles before sitting straight-backed and fastening the seatbelt over my lap. Inside, though, I am shaking, bones rattling against flesh.

Cairn comes to the window as the captain gets behind the wheel. He takes my hand and tells me not to worry. He will get me the best lawyer money could buy. I will be out of there and back home in no time.

I cling to him, to his promise, wanting desperately to believe it, until the car pulls away and I am forced to let go. Someone is faking, though, someone who should be the one being arrested instead of me. Only I am no closer to figuring out who that person is than I was when I started this cockamamie investigation.

Word of my possible guilt must spread quickly. By the time we get to the village, it seems like everyone in County Kirk has come out to see if it is true. If the moor witch has been arrested for murder.

Most just stare, from beside their car meters and through storefront windows. Keeping a safe distance in case I decided to hurl an evil eye at them. A brave few yell expletives. One even throws a rotten tomato that splatters against my window and makes me flinch and Fergus curse.

When we get to the station, he hurries me inside, in case the produce pitcher decides to try his aim at my head.

163

Even after he puts me in a holding cell and locks the sliding bar door before going to hang up his hat, I can still feel their eyes on me. Watching. Judging.

40
A Dangerous Animal

I measure my time in jail by the rising and setting of the sun, which I can see out the window in my small, gray cell. It is too high for me to reach and climb out of, even if I was to drag the single wooden bed underneath it and stand on top, a thought I don't entertain past my first night behind bars.

One day. Two days. Three.

A flurry of different detectives come to question me in a windowless room with a single table and set of chairs while others observe through a two-way mirror. All of them want to know about the night of Myra's murder.

Each time, I tell them the same thing I had Fergus: that the only reason my fingerprints were on the knife that had been used to kill Myra was because I had pulled it out of her. That I had been trying to save her life.

The sessions never last long. At the end of each, the detectives leave, rubbing their heads in frustration, and the captain escorts me back to my cell in silence.

They keep me handcuffed, wrists and ankles, every time they take me out of my cell as if I am a dangerous animal, a flight risk, who might harm someone and then try to flee.

At night, I lie awake, unable to sleep without the sounds of nature around me. Rather than counting sheep, I go through my list of suspects in Lir's disappearance, and now Myra's murder, until their faces blend in my mind's eye.

Rush, with his bloody hammer and bad history with Lir.

Cairn, whose father had wanted a stake in my land so badly he might have been willing to do anything to get it for him.

And D'arcy, who had been the lead detective on Lir's case, yet had been unable to solve it for the first time in his career. Whose fingerprints had been found in Lir's car the night he went missing. Who had spent his life standing in his twin's shadow. Who loved me, had maybe loved me secretly for years. And, most incriminatingly, who had been the only one I'd told about going to see Myra.

No matter how many times I work it out in my head, everything seems to point to D'arcy now. As the hours of my incarceration creep on, the prison feels like a trap. I am a snared animal, vulnerable, helpless to defend myself should he decide to come after me, too. I think of the bottle of poison I'd made, tucked safely away beneath my mattress at home.

A fat lot of good it will do me in here.

And for the first time since hearing the news, I am grateful that the captain had forced him to take a leave of absence from work.

166

41
My Only Other Visitor

The lawyer Cairn had promised to hire shows up at every one of my question-and-answer sessions. He is a tall, slender man, with soft, wrinkled hands, and a salt-and-pepper mustache that matches his full head of wavy hair. He introduces himself to me as Mr. Cleon Walsh. He wears pressed white suits with brightly colored ties, carries a shiny leather briefcase with his initials engraved on it, and spends most of his time interrupting the detectives, waving his hands around and telling me what to and not to say.

The crow is my only other visitor, though Mr. Walsh tells me that Cairn, Rush, D'arcy, my sister, and her boyfriend have all tried to come by. Only he'd sent them away, saying it would only help my case to make me look like a victim.

I want to tell him I am a victim. That he doesn't have to paint me a certain way to show people what is already true. Except he doesn't seem to care about whether I am innocent or guilty, only about the big checks Cairn is writing him, and I don't think he'll listen.

The crow—Lir's crow—shows up every night, right at the stroke of twelve, and stays until the clock chimes the next hour. It doesn't do much, as birds do. Mostly, it preens its feathers. Sometimes it walks back and forth on the windowsill, head bobbing. Others, it sits and stares at me with beady, black eyes.

Still, it is a comfort to have it there. Like a gift from the Morrigan, a sign that I am not alone despite the

167

darkness surrounding me. Every time it leaves, the cavern of loneliness that has been carving its way inside me ever since my arrest gets a little bit bigger.

I have never been good at being alone. After my father left and my mum died, I had secretly dreaded the day my sister would go off to university. Then, when she'd left, I'd at least had Lir, the moor, Nimbus, the animals and plants, and then later, Rush. Here, surrounded by nothing but stone and iron, I feel truly and wholly isolated, cut off from the rest of the world. A balloon left untethered to float into orbit.

I chew on my fingernails and tap my shoe to fill the deafening silence. My skin feels too tight, itchy, as if there are winged, multi-legged things crawling beneath it, and I scratch my forearms until they bleed. Mr. Walsh brings a nurse to wrap up my fingers to keep me from injuring myself further. After that, I stop eating.

If I am going to be found guilty of murder, I reason, I would rather be dead than spend the rest of my life in a cage.

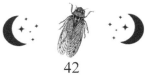

42

The Bee Whisperer

My grandmother was killed for being a witch.

Not that her executioners were entirely wrong.

Annabel De Meath was a bee whisperer, a rare type of nature witch with the ability to speak to, charm, and control bees. Her honey was the finest you could find in any county from Kirk to Donegal. A spoonful could heal the sick. A poultice made from the comb could ease aches and bruises. If you rubbed a little bit on a teething infant's gums, he or she would stop fussing and go right to sleep, and when hardened into candy, it could soften the heart of even the crabbiest curmudgeon.

She was kind and beautiful, the type of girl in her youth who turned heads wherever she went. Yet she wound up married to Merle Hayes, a ne'er-do-well five years her senior with greasy black hair and a disposition meaner than a wet hog, after he knocked her up in the backseat of his old jalopy the summer after her senior year of high school.

They had a shotgun wedding, then Merle moved onto the croft, where he took to drinking himself into an early grave while my grandmother continued her beekeeping. Nine months later, my mother was born.

I don't remember much about my grandmother, save for flashes of red curls poking out from under a sun bonnet and a laugh sweeter than sugar cane. I was only two when she died. But my mother had told me the story of that fateful night enough—normally after I begged her until I was blue in the face, and she relented—that it felt like I had been there.

How the townsfolk had come for her after a mysterious disease wiped out all their crops one harvest. They needed someone to blame for their misfortune, and our family was an easy target.

They dragged her out of bed in the middle of the night, kicking and screaming. My mama managed to get the two of us to safety, climbing down into the old stone well and pulling the hatch closed, where we hung until the men gave up looking for us and left with my grandmother. Barefoot in her nightdress, hair hanging unbound over her shoulders, they hauled her in front of the magistrate.

He spit on her and pronounced her guilty of cavorting with demons. Said that people had reported seeing her talk to bees, telling them not to fertilize the fields so that the crops would fail. Her familiars, he called them.

The constable didn't even wait to give her a proper hearing—not that there would have been anyone willing to speak for her if he had—before he tied a rope around her hands and feet so she couldn't escape then locked her inside a barrel filled with tar. They hauled her through the streets behind a team of horses until she was dead, then burned her body inside its wooden tomb. My mother said they celebrated around the flames long into the next night, dancing and drinking. Three days had passed before she was able to go collect her parent's ashes.

It was only later, when Annabel's death failed to bring back the crops, that the villagers admitted they may have made a mistake. Perhaps the poor harvest had not been the bee whisperer's fault at all, but rather the result of the massive heat wave, which the southern part of Ireland had experienced that year. After all, our county wasn't the only one with farmers who'd lost their crops. They even

170

wrote an official pardon for my grandmother, delivered to our door by courier on fancy stationery.

My mother didn't even bother reading it before she threw it in the fire. No amount of words on paper, she told me, would bring my grandmother back.

Nor did it stop the more superstitious folks in the village from being prejudiced toward our family—hurrying to the other side of the street when they saw us coming and making the sign of the cross if we said hello. As if we wore the mark of what we were on our chests like scarlet brands, and getting too close, much less speaking to us, would result in bad luck.

I have never thought them to be right, until now.

43
The Case of the County Kirk versus Clare Sage

After they hold me for four days, the captain unlocks my cell and leads me down the narrow hall, past the room where they questioned me, and into the small courthouse that adjoined the jail.

Like the latter, the legislative building hasn't seen a renovation since the 1800s. River-like cracks run up the faded stone walls to the rafters above. A permanent layer of dust covers the hardwood floor, capturing my footprints as Fergus guides me to a table near the front of the courtroom. Mr. Walsh is waiting for me there, dressed in another of his garish ties. I don't meet his gaze as I sit down, too afraid of what I might find there, and let the captain handcuff me to the chair.

A cat lays snoozing in one of the tall windows, the sunlight refracting off its tuxedo fur, and I feel a pang at the thought of Nimbus. How I miss her. I hope Rush is feeding her well, and that Cairn is keeping his beastly dog away from her.

Every seat in the wooden pews lining the gallery is packed, filling the air with the unwashed odor of too-many bodies crowded into one space and the *flap-flap* of paper fans waving back and forth in a futile effort to cool the summer heat.

The magistrate is an elderly man with a pointed chin and nose and electric blue eyes that made me think of hellfire. His black robes hang off his skeletal frame like wings, a direct contrast to the full shock of white hair

172

curled over his ears and around his shoulders. It takes me a moment to realize it is a wig.

The captain announces him to the room as "the honorable Jarlath Quinn." I barely have time to rise, a heartbeat behind the rest, before his gnarled fingers grip the gavel and bring it down with a bang, calling us to order as everyone sits again.

"Good morning, good morning." He rustles through a few of the documents on his desk and perches a pair of spectacles atop his nose. "Today we are calling the case of the County Kirk versus Clare Sage in the matter of the murder of Myra Thorpe and the disappearance of Lir Flynn. Council for the Claimant, how does your client plead?"

Cleon put a fatherly hand on my shoulder as he got to his feet, shoulders back and chin up. "Not guilty, Your Honor."

"Thank you, Councilman. All note that the charges against the claimant, Miss Clare Sage, are for indictable offenses, and will therefore be tried by a jury here today. Captain, please swear in the jurors."

I watch through my lashes as the men and women in the box against the far-right wall take their vows to judge what they were about to witness fairly in accordance with the evidence and testimonies presented. I recognize every single one of them.

Ms. Duffy, who'd made my wedding dress only a few weeks before.

Nerdane, one of the girls from Lir's and my class in school I'd cursed with chicken pox.

Ryan, D'arcy's partner when he'd first joined the force.

Lord Geoffrey, Cairn's father.

Lady O'Brian, Cairn's mother.

Father O'Connor, who had been the village priest

173

for as long as anyone could remember. His expression looked as sour today as he raised his right hand as it had on the day of Lir's funeral after I sang my song.

Rukko, the bartender who had served us drinks the night of my bachelorette party. Seeing him up close now, away from the dim lights of the pub, I recognize him from our school's rugby team. The scar he got, from where he took a cleat to the face to make a goal, glares white above his left eyebrow.

Another man whose name tag reads Eames. It takes me a minute to place him before I realize he's the one I ran into in the parking lot the first time I saw the crow.

Rionach, Fergus's daughter. She looks small and slight in her flowing blouse next to the bigger men on either side of her, and I try to remember how old she must be now—eighteen, nineteen perhaps—but can't.

Alani, Rinoach's older sister, and her husband, Dusan. Her belly is full with a child now, and he glances nervously at her every few seconds as if worried these proceedings will be too hard on her in her current state.

Tomas Burke, the grandson of the magistrate who ordered my grandmother's execution. He looks too normal to have come from such a dark bloodline, but I still squirm uncomfortably when he glances my way.

When they finish, the lawyers take the stage for their opening statements. I barely listen as Mr. Walsh speaks about my life, painting a picture of an innocent, hard-working farm girl who has helped many in the village with her skills on more than one occasion. Nor do I pay any attention to the crown prosecutor, a young Mr. Smith who is at least half the age of his opponent based on his cherub cheeks and downy hair. He wears a simple navy suit that goes well with his disarming smile.

I catch the words "witch," "fingerprints," and

174

"opportunity." But my attention is fixed on a golden-brown cicada that has buzzed in through the open door, which the captain had left cracked to combat the worst of the heat. As I watched, it flew circles around the magistrate's head, gossamer wings beating so fast they were a blur, before settling on the rim of his water glass.

"That will be all, gentlemen. Council, you may step down. Prosecution, call your first witness."

"Thank you, Your Honor." Smith tips an imaginary hat. "The prosecution would like to call D'arcy Flynn to the stand."

The familiar name shatters the veil of calm that had settled over me, and my heart skips a beat in my chest. Still, I keep my eyes trained on the bug as D'arcy makes his way to the front of the courtroom. I know if I look at him now, I will fall apart.

"Detective Flynn, you were the first on the scene after the murder of Myra Thorpe. Is that correct?"

"Yes, it is. Clare had called me earlier that night letting me know she was going to meet her, and I was concerned for her well-being. So, I followed her."

"You say you were concerned for her. Why is that?"

"As you know, my brother Lir was recently pronounced dead. He and Clare were engaged to be married before he went missing, and she's taken the loss hard."

"I see. Were you the lead detective on that case as well?"

"I was."

"Then perhaps you can clear up something for the court. I have here two sets of fingerprints kindly provided by your superior officer. One was taken from the handle of the knife used to stab Miss Thorpe. The other was found on the steering wheel of Mr. Flynn's car the night he went missing. Could you please read aloud the name printed at

175

the bottom here of the person to who these prints belong to?"

I can almost hear D'arcy's expression harden as he turns to look up at the magistrate. "Forgive me, Your Honor, but I fail to see how that information is relevant to this hearing since both sets of fingerprints have already been dismissed as circumstantial evidence."

Mr. Quinn arched an eyebrow at the CP. "Well?"

"I assure you, I have a point."

"So moved. Detective Flynn, please answer the question."

A beat.

"Both sets of fingerprints belong to Clare Sage, but as I stated…"

The young man cut him off with a flick of his fingers as he snapped the folder in his hand closed. "That will be all, Detective. Thank you. No further questions."

"Very well. Council, your witness."

Cleon's bones creaked as he rose and approached the bench. "Detective Flynn, let me be the first to apologize on behalf of this court for the loss of your brother. I am sure it must be difficult to continue having his case dredged up repeatedly." He looked pointedly over his shoulder at the prosecutor, who tightened his jaw.

"Thank you. I appreciate it."

"Of course. And speaking of your brother, isn't it true that, being his fiancée and all, Miss Sage had been in his car on numerous occasions before his unfortunate disappearance?"

"Absolutely."

"Hmm. Not only that but weren't there other prints found in Mr. Flynn's car during the initial investigation as well?"

"Yes, several, among them my own, my parents,

176

and my younger brother's. All of us had reason to have been in Lir's car under normal circumstances, which is why the prints were dismissed as not being related to the case." He looked directly at the prosecutor as he said this, who didn't appear the least bit ruffled by the statement.

I knew why.

It didn't matter what the facts said. All he needed to do was plant the seed of doubt in everyone's mind, then let their natural prejudice against me do the rest.

"Of course." Mr. Walsh nodded as if this made perfect sense. "Let us move on then to the night of Myra Thorpe's murder. You stated earlier that you received a call from the defendant earlier in the evening telling you where she was going."

"That's right."

"An odd thing for someone planning a murder to do, wouldn't you agree?"

"Yes."

"Then tell me, Detective, why did Miss Sage call your home that night to make you aware of her plans?"

"Because I'd asked her to. Clare wasn't as willing as the rest of us to give up on finding out what happened to Lir, and I was worried about her biting off more than she could chew."

"As would anyone grieving a lost love. I can only imagine the pain she must have felt, must still be feeling, at not having closure." He cast a sympathetic look at the juror's box, and instinctively I realized this was my only chance at salvation. If my lawyer could make the jury feel sorry enough for me, they might acquit me. "What exactly did Miss Sage say in her message?"

"She told me that she thought Myra might know something about Lir's disappearance that the police didn't, and she was going to ask her about it."

177

"Which is why you went after her."

"Yes."

"Around what time would you say it was when you left for Galway?"

"About eight-thirty p.m. I got off shift a little after eight, went straight home, and found the message waiting on my machine. I headed back out immediately."

"Please describe in as much detail as possible exactly what you saw when you arrived at the tavern."

"Well—" D'arcy's Adam's apple bobbed up and down. "I heard screaming first. That's what alerted me to the alley and not the front door. I recognized Clare's voice. She was yelling for help. She sounded terrified. By the time I got there, she was unconscious from what looked like a blow to the back of the head. Myra was dead from multiple stab wounds to the gut and one which severed her right arm. The murder weapon was on the ground beside her."

"You saw no one else? Heard no footsteps running away, no doors slamming, or the sound of a getaway car?"

"Unfortunately not. However, the alley led onto the main street with plenty of traffic, both vehicular and on foot, and there were several other businesses besides the bar with back entrances near the dumpsters. Any of these could have provided an easy escape for a perpetrator."

"Thank you, Detective. Your insight has been truly invaluable. I have one more question we must address. When your captain asked Miss Sage why her fingerprints were on the knife used to kill Miss Thorpe, what did she say?"

"That she had only touched it to pull it out to try and save her life."

"In an effort to save her life." Mr. Walsh swept his hands out toward the room in a "there you have it" motion before bowing his head at D'arcy. "Thank you, Detective

178

Flynn. No further questions, Your Honor."

44
Guilty or Not Guilty?

The rest of the hearing goes much the same, with the crown prosecutor trying to paint me as an evil murderer and Cleon doing everything that he can to rebut each attack and make me look like a victim. Some testimonies, like Arleen's, Rush's, and Cairn's, are easy the way D'arcy's had been. They all have only good things to say about me, all attest to my grief at Lir's disappearance, even reinforce my alibi for the night he'd gone missing. I am grateful for the help, though the little voice in the back of my mind can't help but wonder which one of them is lying. Others, like the doctor who had treated my head wound, Myra's former boss from the bar, and the superintendent of Lir's apartment building, are a little harder.

The doctor cannot say with certainty what type of object had caused the injury, to which Mr. Smith purports that this leaves the possibility that it could have been self-inflicted. And while both the manager and superintendent had not seen anything suspicious happen between myself and Lir or myself and Myra that might have pointed to my guilt, they do verify that they had seen me at both places. At the very least, he argues, this put me at the scene of the crimes, although my lawyer insists that I'd had a plausible reason to be there both times that had nothing to do with the murder.

Things do not get really bad, however, until the CP begins to question the townspeople about my character.

Mr. Cunningham, whose blue-ribbon heifer had

given sour milk two years ago after I treated her for a bad case of foot and mouth. A side effect of the marigold leaves, I had told him when he confronted me about it, which would go away in a few days once the herb was out of her system. Only he hadn't listened, claiming I had cursed the beast, and he had slaughtered it to prevent any black magic effects from spreading to the rest of his herd.

Old Mr. Murphy from the grocery, who must have been pushing ninety now. He tells everyone the story of how I had stolen candy from him as a child. "Once a thief and a liar, always a thief and a liar."

Miss McKinley, my old grade school teacher, looks just as pinched and stern in her high-necked dress as I remember, though a good bit more wrinkled now. She recounts the mysterious ailment that had befallen the girls in my class who had picked on me.

Alice, who backs up Miss McKinley and says I made her sick, then went on to declare that I'd also used a love spell to steal Lir from her when we were younger. Never mind that they had never even seriously dated.

I feel every slur they hurl from their lips like the crack of a whip—witch, devil woman, whore, saboteur—until my skin is numb and raw.

Mr. Walsh deflects every one of their testimonies as allegations. Surely, he protests, veins bulging at the side of his neck as he pounds a fist on the table, we are not such a primitive people as to still believe these types of whimsical fantasies are possible, much less credible in a court of law. The magistrate sustains each one. Except I know the damage is already done.

No matter what I do, or what my lawyer says, the people of County Kirk will only ever see me one way: as the moor witch. As something to be feared.

"The prosecution rests, your honor."

181

"Does the council have any further witnesses?"

"Just one." Cleon rises to his feet, the fingertips of his right hand stroking the edge of his tie. "If it pleases the court, I would like to call the claimant, Miss Clare Sage, to the stand."

This time, the whispers in the room reach a crescendo that lasts almost a full minute before the magistrate regains control. I barely feel it as the captain unlocks my cuffs and leads me to the witness box. The seat is hard and cold beneath me as if the warmth of the day can't touch it.

The magistrate peers down at me kindly, and I force myself to meet his gaze. "Miss Sage, you understand that you have the right to refuse to testify on your behalf, and if you choose to step down, it cannot be used against you.

I swallow. My tongue feels dry as sandpaper. "I do. But I want to."

"Very well." He sits back and steeples his fingers with a nod at Mr. Walsh. "You may proceed."

"Thank you, Your Honor." My lawyer approaches the stand. "Miss Sage, please state your full name for the court."

"Clare Sage, sir."

"Thank you. Where were you on the night of August tenth?"

"I had taken a train to Galway, to meet Myra at the bar where she worked."

"And what was your purpose for meeting with Miss Thorpe?"

"I thought she might know something about Lir's death that would help solve the case."

He arches his eyebrows, though we'd been over this before at least half a dozen times. "And did she?"

"I-I don't know. She was killed before I could find

182

out."

"Thank you, Miss Sage. No further questions, Your Honor."

"Your witness." The magistrate gestures to the CP, and I watch him make his way toward me. He moves like a snake through tall grass. My pulse jumps at the base of my throat like a sand midge, keeping time with the hands of the clock on the wall.

"Miss Sage, can you describe your relationship with the murder victim?"

"I didn't have one. I had only met her once before when D'arcy and I went to Lir's apartment to collect his things."

"Interesting. Yet somehow you came up with the idea that she retained information about your fiancé's case that she had not made known to the police. How is that, if you had hardly spoken to her?"

"She was in Lir's class. If something had happened to him while he was in the city that led to his disappearance, she might have known about it."

"Mr. Flynn had many schoolmates though, did he not? What, pray tell, made this one so special?"

I falter, the answer I had been about to give slipping off my tongue like an eel. I feel that brush of feather lightness again, as if there is something hidden in the recesses of my mind, something important, something I cannot, or will not, remember. A dark foreboding fills me without word or explanation, and this time, I do not retreat. I reach for it, wanting, needing to grab ahold and pull it into the open air with a hunger I do not understand but know I must obey. Only try as I might, it darts away whenever I get too close, as fleeting and ghostly as quicksilver, just out of reach, before fading back into nothingness altogether.

I can feel all the eyes in the room on me and realize

183

that they are still waiting for my answer. I clear my throat self-consciously. "I-I don't know. I just had a feeling."

"A feeling," he repeats, giving the jury a meaningful look. "Like the one you had about Mr. Flynn's disappearance being a death, you mean?"

When I don't answer right away, too stunned and confused to do anything but gape at him, he presses on with all the force of a freight train. "Earlier, you stated that you sought out Miss Thorpe because you believed she knew something pertinent to your fiancée's death. However, Detective Flynn stated earlier that you were opposed to accepting the change from a missing person's case because you didn't want to accept that he was gone. Isn't that correct?"

I feel Lir's ghost hovering behind me, breathing down my neck. I look around, searching for some sight of him, but there is nothing there. "No. I mean, yes, I..."

"And isn't it also a fact that you were the last person to see both Mr. Flynn and Miss Thorpe alive?"

"Yes, I was, but..."

"Then please explain, if you will, this sudden change of heart and why you were so eager to meet with the victim that you left home in the middle of the night if you weren't directly responsible for Mr. Flynn's demise and planning hers as well?"

He spins toward the jury, not bothering to wait for my answer. "Let us not forget, ladies and gentlemen, that this woman loved Lir Flynn, and crimes of passion are the most common. After all, Hell hath no fury like a woman scorned."

This is too much for me to take. My temper flares. Forgetting where I am, I leap to my feet, mouth open to shout in my defense even as self-doubt swirls through my mind like storm clouds, filling the gaps where the answers

184

to his questions ought to be but, for some reason, are not. As if something, or someone, has erased them.

I couldn't have killed Lir! I want to say. It wasn't me. It couldn't have been me! I loved him. Surely, I would remember something like that, wouldn't I?

I recall the image of my darker self in the mirror, the eerie, inhuman smile on her face and the bloody blade in her hand. I haven't seen her again since that day, for which I am grateful. No mirrors in prison. Yet I cannot shake the feeling that she is still there, lurking on the edge of my consciousness, waiting to reveal something that I both desperately need to know and am terrified to learn.

The chair legs scrape loudly across the floor as Cleon stands before I can speak and condemn myself further in the eyes of the court. "Objection, Your Honor! The prosecution is leading the witness."

"On the contrary. I am merely trying to illustrate that there are gaps in the defense's story, and Miss Sage's testimony could bring them to light."

"What a load of bollocks!"

"Gentlemen, refrain yourselves!"

I shiver, hugging my arms as I listen to them abandon all pretense of decorum and argue. The cicada's feet track through the water droplets clinging to the glass as it walks along the rim. I cannot tell the truth. No one would believe that Lir's ghost had come to me, asking me to avenge his death. They would think I was crazy and lock me back up again. Maybe for good this time.

Maybe they should.

A caw comes from overhead, and I look up to see the crow perched among the rafters. Its beady eyes fix on me as it ruffles its feathers. The cat must see it too, making her feel a little less like I'm going crazy, because it rises from its slumber, arches it back, and stalks toward it on

185

silent paws. When it makes a leap, trying to catch it, the bird flies to another perch. Its beak opens as if in laughter.

"Overruled. Miss Sage, please answer the question."

My mind races as I look around, trying to come up with a way out of this as he raises the cup to his lips. I watch as the cicada clings to the side rather than fly away, expecting him to notice. Only, all his attention is on me, and he swallows both insect and water in one large gulp. I see where it gets stuck halfway down his trachea, a winged bulge through his skin, like a second Adam's apple.

The magistrate chokes, face turning red, then purple, as his eyes grow wide. He flings his hands to his neck, letting the glass fall. It shatters, the sound like a gunshot, and the courtroom erupts into madness.

Mr. Walsh rushes to give Mr. Quinn the Heimlich as the prosecutor jumps back, pointing at me and shouting that here was the proof. I had done this. I was a witch, and they were all next. The crowd stampedes toward the door, driven by fear at his words. Their screams bounce off the walls. Mr. Cunningham and Mr. Murphy rush at me, and I can see the intent in their eyes. To grab me. To beat me. To drag me into the street like their ancestors had my grandmother and hang me to stop the spell they think I have cast. I tense, bracing for the moment their hands close around my throat.

Only it never comes, because the captain draws his baton and steps between us, swinging it at the closet man. He and his companion skid to a halt, the weapon narrowly missing their heads, and several ladies scream again. The magistrate, who is still flushed and wheezing but alive thanks to Cleon's quick thinking, crawls back into his chair and bangs his gavel.

"Order! There will be order in this court. This is not

186

a witchcraft trial. It is a murder hearing, and I want any such claims stricken from the record."

"But, Your Honor…!"

"Silence, Smith," Mr. Quinn snaps, and the prosecutor's mouth slams shut. "I expected more from someone who studied law at Oxford than a smear campaign. Did you think I would let you get away with dragging the defendant's name through the mud by playing on folkloric superstitions?"

The young man's cheeks bloom pink, yet he presses on. "You said…"

"Forget what I said. My previous ruling is retracted. All further questioning of the claimant is sustained, and I am ordering the jury to refrain from using any accusations of witchcraft, speculative or otherwise, in their decision. I will not have a mockery made of this hearing, and unless you want me to find you in contempt, I suggest you stand down."

The CP's voice sounded as if it had been raked over hot coals. "Very well. The prosecution rests."

"The council for the claimant also rests, Your Honor," Mr. Walsh said, doing a decent job of looking humble. Still, I catch the smug smirk he shoots his opponent as he returns to his seat.

"Good. Miss Sage, you may step down."

Shaking as the adrenaline in my veins dies down now that the excitement is over, I let the captain help me back to my table as the lawyers give their closing arguments. His hand at my elbow is warm and comforting, and I recall how he had moved to defend me from the mob.

Maybe he isn't such a bad guy after all.

Cleon's speech is what I'd expected: the story of a poor, misunderstood girl accused of a crime she hadn't committed without any true supporting evidence based

187

solely on prejudice. Smith does his best to refute it, but the wind has been knocked out of his sails, and without being able to use the witchcraft angle, his words fall flat.

The magistrate calls for an adjournment while the jury deliberates, and people get up and mill around, talking among themselves about the events of the day. The cat wakes and stretches, arching its back, before hopping down from the ledge and trotting off in search of a mouse to hunt for its dinner. I stay seated, eyes on the rafters, even when Mr. Walsh asks if I need to use the loo or want something to drink. But the crow is gone, undoubtedly flown off in all the commotion, and does not return.

The jury is only gone for about thirty minutes. When they come back, Ms. Duffy hands the magistrate a folded piece of paper. He reads it with a blank face, then looks at me.

"Will the claimant please rise?"

I do, knees knocking together so hard I am sure everyone can hear it. What would the ruling be? Guilty, or not guilty? Cleon stands beside me, hands clasped neatly above his belt.

"In the matter of the County Kirk versus Clare Sage, the jury finds the claimant not guilty of all charges. My learned friends, thank you for your time. You are free to go."

A wave of overwhelming disbelief washes over me, crushing my lungs and blurring my vision. It is a trick. I am sure of it, and I search the magistrate and juror's faces for signs of dishonesty. Yet I find none, only pity and a few sad, kind smiles that make my chest hurt. When the captain unlocks my handcuffs with a murmur of apology for what I have been through, I can no longer hold myself together, and I collapse, relief turning my bones to liquid.

Mr. Walsh catches me. His lapel is rough against

my cheek, and he murmurs into my ear as he pats my back, "There, there. Do no' worry, Lass. I've got ya. It's all over now."

The captain hands him a bag containing my few belongings—the shoelaces and ring he had taken from me when he booked me. If I ever need anything, he says, I should not hesitate to let him know.

I want to thank him for all of his kindness to me over these past few days, but I cannot seem to find my voice. I hope the tears in my eyes are gratitude enough. They must be, because he gives me a small smile and touches two fingers to the brim of his hat before moving away. Then Arlene is there, and D'arcy, and Cairn, and Rush, even Jake, wonderful, solid, and familiar, folding me in their arms, and I let them usher me away from the lawyer and out the door.

The sun hurts my eyes when I step outside, making me squint from too many days spent indoors. Yet the air smells fresh, like freedom. My family helps me into the waiting wagon, where Rhiannon turns her head enough to nuzzle me, and take me home. When I get there, I go straight to the oak tree in the backyard, kneel on the earth with Nimbus curling around my legs and the cicadas buzzing around my head, and finally let out the tears I have been holding in, back where I belong.

45
Brigid

I see her this morning. Brigid the rabbit. I am bent over in the field, collecting the first of the heather to grind for teas, tinctures, and oils, when I hear a soft, thumping footstep. The past few days have been a struggle to get back into my routine after being locked up. I still am not sleeping well, my dreams plagued with images of bloody weapons and glinting pocket watches when I do drift off. I look up, skin tingling, and there she is, nearly as tall as my knee, her sunshine-colored fur shimmering in the soft light of dawn, the same shade it had been when she was still human.

Her ears are pricked, whiskers twitching as she listens for any sound of danger. For a moment, her bright blue eyes meet mine, seeming to glow with an inner power, and I forget how to breathe. Then, the dog is there, bursting through the rows of plants with a thunderous bark.

How we hadn't heard him coming, I don't know.

Brigid pivots on her heels, preparing to run. But he is too fast, snatching her up in his powerful jaws before she can escape.

The rabbit screams a horrible, strangled cry that I echo, clawing at my neck, feeling the dog's teeth sink into her delicate flesh, severing my tie to her power like an umbilical cord. Cairn is there, yelling commands, pulling Mas off her. But it is too late. Her throat is a mangled mess of blood, fur, and flesh, her eyes dull, cloudy, and unseeing, and I sink to my knees, wailing over her lifeless body, as the cicadas join in.

46
Slipping into Madness

I sit in the field with the rabbit's body long after Cairn has taken his pet away. Nimbus has made herself scarce, probably afraid that she will be next. Rush comes by and offers to help me inside. I send him away to finish repairing the fence, unable to be near another person.

When I touch its fur, the golden strands are cold and stiff, as if it has been dead for far longer than a few hours. I press my palms to the ground, try to feel a connection to the earth, to call forth a tree, a flower, a blade of grass, anything. The soil has become as empty and lifeless as my ancestor's animal form, though, and there is no response.

I build a small pyre out of sticks and weeds and place Brigid on top. Without magic, I am forced to use two rocks to start a fire. I work at it until long after the moon has risen and the stars have opened their eyes, striking the stones together until, at last, they spark. I sit back, cupping my blistered hands together.

The fire catches quickly on the kindling, spreading to Brigid's prone form. I watch as she burns, flames dancing across my vision until they swim, morphing into violent flashes of red and black. I squeeze my eyes shut until they disappear. Still, the memory of them lingers, making me feel shaken, my skin stretched too tight over muscle and bone.

I wait until the blaze has died down completely, reduced to ash, then go into the house and climb into bed. The lanterns have been put out already, their wicks doused.

Cairn is asleep, the deep, even sound of his breathing a balm to my wounded soul. Only I can't drift off, not that night or the next. The buzzing of the cicadas has grown exceedingly louder, making it impossible for me to rest. Worse, I think I hear a stirring, scratching beneath the dirt as if some otherworld monster is trying to dig his way to the surface.

I even ask Cairn about it, on the third morning at breakfast, but he merely looks at me oddly and asks me if I'm feeling all right.

One week after Mas killed the rabbit, I am on my last leg. No amount of tea can rid me of the sheer exhaustion I feel, though I have tried them all. Every nerve ending in my body is on edge. My eyelids, my limbs, and even my teeth feel heavy, and I keep thinking I see my darker mirror self from the corner of my gaze. Yet every time I look, stomach churning sickly and skin slick with dread, there is nothing there, only my ordinary shadow standing tall and thin against the wall.

Without my magic, I feel spread too thin, my mind a jumble of incoherent thoughts and memories. I am no longer certain of what's real and what's not. I worry that I am slipping into madness.

47
Song of the Cicadas

D'arcy comes to call one morning shortly after breakfast. I had almost forgotten about Myra's ongoing murder investigation in the haze after losing Brigid. Yet instinctively I know that is what he is here for by the way he makes his way up the walk, mouth in a grim, no-nonsense line, badge pinned to his shirt, notepad, and pencil in hand to where I stand in the front yard, hanging the last of the dyed wool on the line to dry. The damp, rich green, indigo, and scarlet linens drip onto the grass, flapping in the breeze rolling off the ocean like the wings of captive doves trying to break free.

I am surprised to see him and say as much.

The captain, he explains, decided to give him the case because he'd been first on the scene, and "He was tired of dealing with the out-of-towners. Plus, he thinks it will be good to focus on something else."

I agree. He does look better, his uniform clean and pressed, his hair combed, his eyes bright and alert. I am glad if a bit envious. My head feels foggy, and little lights are sparking at the edges of my vision, making my teeth ache. I see the way he looks at me when I let him in, glancing askance at my wild mane that hasn't been brushed in days and wrinkled dress. My hands stained a motley of multicolored hues from the dyes. A woman unhinged. But he is a gentleman and doesn't say anything as I invite him to sit down while I fix us some tea.

I add a few drops of the poison to his cup when he isn't looking, then bring the drinks over to the table along with a plate of blackberry scones.

He traces a finger around the edge of the saucer but makes no move to drink it. I watch, willing him to pick it up, only half-listening as he tells me that the coroner has concluded that Myra was killed by multiple stab wounds. That her arm was cut off after she was already dead, and it is most likely the killer was still in the alley when I found her and knocked me out to escape unseen. I already know all of this.

When he flips open his little black notebook and starts asking me questions about that night, I do my best to answer like I did the other detectives. But the answers come out jumbled, a tangle of words I can't quite unravel.

Finally, he gives up. "This is getting us nowhere. I'm sorry to have bothered you, Clare. I know this can't be easy for you, after everything you've been through this year. I'm just trying to tie up loose ends." He fiddles with the handle of his teacup. I can tell there is more he wants to say as it clacks against the rim of the saucer. Some of the liquid spills onto the table, a waste of poison. "There's one other thing. Do you have any idea why your fingerprints were the only ones on the knife?"

"No." I blink, my brain slow, sluggish, as if mired in mud. "It-it doesn't make any sense. I only touched it to pull it out. The killer would have had to stab her."

"They could have worn gloves, especially if it was premeditated like the evidence suggests. Are you sure you didn't see anything, hear a voice or specific gait, smell perfume, anything that could help us pin down a suspect?"

"No." That damned dog is barking again, making it hard to concentrate. A muscle twitches at the corner of my eye, and I press a finger to it, trying to remain calm. "Just

195

shadows and garbage, and blood. There was so much blood." My stomach roils at the memory of it, the sharp copper scent, the dark red stains on my clothes and hands. I take a drink of my tea, hoping it will wash it down. But it only makes it worse. "What about Rush? The hammer I sent you? The red on the tip..."

"Was blood," D'arcy finishes, and my heart leaps into my throat. I nearly knock his tea to the floor. Was I wrong this whole time, and it was my repair person I should have been focused on instead? "You were right. Just not Lir's. It was Rush's blood. Probably he hit his thumb with it one day during a repair job and never bothered to clean it off."

"Oh." I sit back in my chair slowly, hands fidgeting in my lap.

D'arcy sighs, runs both hands through his hair. I can already see the frustration lining his face at hitting another dead end. The fear that this case will wind up like his brother's—unsolved. I wish I could help him. Only I can't.

"None of this makes any sense. Myra was a simple girl. Went to school and her job at the bar, then home by ten every night like clockwork. She was an only child, orphaned when she was nineteen, didn't have any enemies to speak of, no boyfriend or jealous ex, and her small circle of friends had nothing but good things to say about her. I suppose it could have been a robbery, but nothing seems to be missing."

He keeps talking, speculating about how it's possible I scared the thief away before they had the chance to steal her wallet or jewelry. I can hardly hear him, though. The dog is barking louder now, the sound almost frenetic, and I get to my feet abruptly, my chair scraping across the floor.

Ignoring D'arcy's questions of, "Clare? What's

196

wrong? Where are you going?" I stride to the door and throw it open.

The song of the cicadas hits me like a sonic boom, so loud it nearly drowns out the dog, making me stagger. I have to lean against the door post for a minute to get my bearings. There are so many of them this year, I think. In fact, there were a lot more than normal last year, too, and the year before that, and every year since the night my life changed forever. Their tiny brown bodies swarm over the old oak so that its branches seem to ripple with movement. Then I am moving again, around the side of the house and through the backyard with purposeful strides.

D'arcy chases after me, concern in his voice. But I ignore him. I am going to kill that beast, strangle it with my bare hands if I have to.

Mas is at the foot of the oak tree, Nimbus half hidden among the leaves overhead, near the spot where his master fell when the crow attacked him. At first, I think he has cornered her there, much like Rush did the bird, and lightning shoots behind my eyes. Then I realize he is digging, not even looking at the cat, eyes focused on the soil at the base of the tree as more cicadas, roots, and clods of dirt fly past his paws.

My jaw unhinges, an inhuman cry bursting from my lungs as I rush at him, hands outstretched. Cairn is already there, both hands wrapped around his collar, shouting commands as he tries to drag him away. But the dog will not be moved. And as I near, I can see it is too late.

There, in the hole he has made, lie the remnants of a corpse. Its khaki pants and white button-up shirt hang off its skeletal frame in rags.

Its skull is caved in at the back as if he has been struck in the head with a heavy object. Dirt and blood crusts beneath broken fingernails next to deep gauges in the

197

earth where it tried to claw its way to freedom before its air ran out. One of its eyes is missing. The other stares up at us, empty and unseeing, its mouth open in a silent scream as cicadas swarm in and out of its gaping orifices. They have been nesting in them, the flesh of its jaw half rotted away on the left side, revealing the stark white bone beneath.

Cairn and D'arcy gape at it in shock, no longer concerned with controlling the dog or catching me. The former is silent now, his job done, and sits back on its haunches at its master's side, tongue drooping happily.

I knew keeping him would be a mistake.

D'arcy is the first one to recover his senses and climbs down into the hole. Brushing the worst of the insects aside, he reaches into the dead man's back pocket, one hand covering his nose against the smell, and pulls something out.

A wallet.

He opens it, reads the name printed there in small black letters silently to himself. But then, he doesn't need to speak them aloud. I already know what they say.

He looks up at me, forehead so furrowed his eyes are touching. "It's Lir. But how...?"

I know what he wants to ask. What he wants me to say. How did Lir's body wind up buried in my backyard? Who could have done this? Except I can't give him the answers he wants. Words slip and fall on my tongue before they can reach my lips as a memory—and it is a memory, I realize with a sick kind of horror, one that I have spent the last seven years repressing, until I somehow managed to all but forget it had happened—pushes its way to the front of my mind.

48
Blood and Bone, Heart and Stone

Lir and I stand beneath the oak tree.

It is night, and the moon cascades silver beams in his hair, making it appear gray instead of chestnut brown. He has a suitcase in one hand, his keys in the other. He is leaving for school, he says. But there is something not right in the way his eyes don't quite meet mine when he kisses me goodbye, lips dry and stagnant against my cheek when we used to barely be able to keep our hands off one another. Hidden words on his tongue that he's too afraid to say out loud.

Things have been different between us lately, it's true. The months spent apart while he is at university and I am here tending to the croft that will be our home, where we will raise our children, have driven a rift between us that gets harder and harder to close each time he comes to visit. Still, we have always been able to talk to each other about anything.

I demand to know what's wrong, certain that it is something trivial and foolish, like worrying over exams. Then I can reassure him that he is far smarter than his professors, that all the late-night studying we have done will pay off. And we will laugh about it, both feeling better for having gotten it off his chest.

Instead, he tells me that he's met someone. The girl, Myra, was in his study group last semester. How she is funny and kind, and gentle, and that he loves her. Wants to be with her, and he was waiting for the right time to tell me. To end things between us. That he didn't want me to find out like this. That he's sorry. Only I can no longer hear him.

A strange hum has begun to build in my ears, like the buzz of the cicadas that emerge from the ground here every year. There are few left now. Summer is almost over. Soon, the weather will chill, covering the trees with a layer of frost, and they will burrow deep into the ground to wait out the winter. Still, the thought reminds me of the story of my ancestor, Brigid, and how her love for Torin drove her to turn him into the first of the bugs so that his endless cycle of shedding his ancient skin and being reborn anew ensured they might always be together.

I see my father striding up the road, hair gleaming in the noonday sun and a rucksack on his back. When he reached the bend in the road, he looked back, and lifted a hand in farewell toward my sister and me where we sat on the fence, our faces sticky with plums, before continuing on.

I see my mother lying in bed, unnaturally pale and thin as a rail, a blood-stained handkerchief pressed to her lips. The coughs racked her body, and rattled her lungs until at last, she fell still.

I see my sister, dressed in a sharp outfit, smart suitcase in one hand and college acceptance letter clutched in the other, boarding the train to Galway. The whistle is loud, and the puffing of the engine fills the station with smoke. She waves through the window of her compartment, grinning from ear to ear until she is too far down the tracks for me to see her.

Everyone I ever loved has abandoned me until the only sure thing in my life was the croft. The slow, easy turn of the seasons. The sowing and reaping. The return of the rabbits and cicadas at the same time every year. And I find

200

myself wondering if there is something wrong with me, something dark, raw, and wild, that makes them not want to stay.

Even Lir had gone off to the city for better education, though he'd promised to come back. To start a life here with me. Only now, it seems, he's changed his mind. Found someone else to be his bride.

I picture her, what she must look like, prim, proper, and soft. All the things that I am not. Imagine her sitting in Lir's drawing room, hosting afternoon teas for the fine ladies of the village, a gaggle of curly-haired, blue-eyed children running around at her feet, while I peddle my wares in the street. Envision the way that Lir will bend down and kiss her gently when he comes home from work each night, how they will lie in bed together, warm and content in each other's arms, while I grow old and gray by the fire, alone save for Rush and the animals.

Tears break over the crest of my lashes, and I grab onto him, begging him not to do this. I love him, I cry. I will always love him, better and stronger than she can. We are meant to be, he and I, two creatures cut from the same stone. He cannot leave me alone!

But now that he has said his piece, his mind is made up. My pleas are ignored, twisting the mouth that once kissed the most intimate parts of my body, that whispered everlasting vows of devotion in my ear, into a hard line of pity and revulsion. When he turns to go, something in me, some tenuous thread that was always drawn a little too tight, snaps.

Anger replacing my sorrow, I snatch up a rock from the path to the gate, cutting my palm on the sharp edge, and bring it down against the back of his head. It is a true blow, and a hard one, and he falls to the ground, bleeding and still. He is not dead, though, merely unconscious. His chest rises and falls with even breaths.

I grab him by the ankles and drag him around the house to the backyard, where I use my magic to open a hole in the earth beneath the oak tree. I roll him in, listen with satisfaction to the thud of his body when it hits the bottom.

He used to climb this tree as a boy, would taunt me from its branches, knowing that I was unable to come up after him—I have always been afraid of heights—until I would stamp my foot and threaten to tell our parents. Then he would scramble down, fist full of catkins, and present them to me as an apology. It is a fitting spot for his eternal resting place, here, with the cicadas a symbol of the same undying love that Brigid and Torin shared as we do.

The stones I need to line his bed with to ensure he is never able to leave it are too heavy for me to lift. Another gust of power pulls them free and floats them down into the hole, where I pack them neatly, side by side, walling him in.

He wakes up before I am finished. First confusion, then panic tinges his eyes when he realizes where he is and what I am doing. He tries to climb out, hands scrabbling uselessly at the sides of his tomb. I have dug the pit too deep, and he begins to call out to me instead. Begs me to let him out, promises that he will stay. That he made a mistake. That I am the only one he wants.

I do not believe him. If I were to let him out now, he would go back to her and tell the police what I'd done. His brother would come and take me from my home, lock me away in a hospital where they dress you in sterile gowns and all of your meals come through a tube. I would never see him again. Wouldn't be able to shield him from Myra's charms, make him realize how wrong she is for him.

Better that he stay here with me, where we can both

be safe. Where we can both be together.

He curses me, in the end, as I place the last stones over his face. But the ground muffles the cruelty of his words, leaving me with a strange feeling of peace and completion. It is done. And now, thanks to Lir, I will never be alone.

I pack his luggage into the trunk and drive his car to the gas station half a mile from the train station. There, I buy a cup of coffee from the elderly night shift clerk behind the counter. Black, just how he likes it. A simple mixture of hallucinogenic herbs blown into her eyes and a few muttered words are enough to convince her that she is seeing him instead of me. I pay cash, then return to the car, put the coffee in the cupholder without taking a sip, and drive another mile down the road, where I leave it, engine still idling, next to a crooked stop sign and walk home.

The first night, Lir's cries keep me awake, shouts of "Please! Someone, help me! Get me out of here!" as he beats his fists uselessly against the walls of his underground tower. After the second, his voice has grown hoarser, the slap of his hands against the stone feebler. By the third, they have quieted completely. On the fourth day, I hire Rush to help me on the croft. Once anyone realizes he is missing, autumn has already arrived, freezing the ground, turning his prison into a natural refrigerator, preserving his flesh, and getting rid of any smell that might have alerted D'arcy and the other detectives who come nosing around looking for him, asking questions about the night he disappeared.

And they do come sniffing, their suspicions all pointed at me at first. Even D'arcy, though I can tell he is only doing what is expected of him. But I still have the ring Lir gave me when he first left for school, a small gold band with a single morganite stone at its center that he swore he would replace with a diamond when he came back to marry me, and no one except me knew about Myra. Or so I thought until she told me later about the fight between D'arcy and Lir.

The younger twin must have found out about his brother's secret girlfriend and tried to talk him out of leaving me. When he disappeared, and I still had the ring, he no doubt thought Lir had listened.

Besides, men tend to see what they want to see, so sure about the superiority of their abilities that they fool themselves into believing they can't be hoodwinked. Who would ever think that the young, teary-eyed fiancée, sick with worry over her missing love and struggling to keep her family farm going, was actually behind the whole thing?

So, I told my lies, and I told them well. After a while, I even started to convince myself they were real. That what had happened with Lir had been another bad dream, brought on by the stress of his disappearance and my fear of abandonment. Still, some nights, after Rush had fallen asleep on his cot in the barn, I would sneak out into the backyard, lay down beneath the oak tree, and press my ear to the ground, listening, ears straining for the telltale beat of Lir's heart. Sometimes, I thought I heard it, a tiny flutter, like that of an infant in the womb. Others, I knew it was only the sound of the grass growing, spreading its roots deep beneath the soil.

In the end, that went away too, and I fell deeper into the deception of my lies, until they became so interwoven with my reality that, after seven years, I could no longer tell one from the other. Covering the mirrors had helped further, preventing me from facing myself and what I had done. Even when I saw his ghost, when he pleaded with me to let him go, I believed that someone else had killed him.

Of course, that part wasn't totally a lie. Someone

204

else had stolen him from me.

I shouldn't have killed Myra. I never planned to. Once Lir was effectively separated from her, there was no reason to get rid of her. But when I saw her, standing there in the hallway outside his apartment, clearly mourning him in a way that she had no right to do, with the ring he had given her still on her hand, some deep, dark part of me reared its head with a yawn, unable to rest again until she was dead.

So, I visited her work under the guise of uncovering Lir's murderer, waited until she went to dump the trash, then followed her outside and stabbed her to death with my mother's athame before she even had time to scream. I cut off her left arm for good measure, a kind of permanent severance of her final connection to Lir. Then I staged the scene so that it looked as if I had only stumbled upon it, not caused it.

That part was harder to forget, though the blow I gave myself when I slammed my head into the wall helped.

Still, I could have gotten away with it. Blamed it on Rush or D'arcy, either of whom could have stolen the knife from my house. Might have even been able to forget about Lir and be happy here with Cairn, if it hadn't been for that stupid dog. First killing the rabbit and severing my ties to my magic, then digging up Lir's body. Only now, staring at the stark, ugly proof in front of me, the weight of the guilt squeezing my bones, snapping them like twigs—*blood and bone, heart and stone*—I can no longer deny what I have done.

49
Free at Last

"Something obvious." I meet D'arcy's gaze solemnly, let him see the truth written plain on my face. I watch as his expression morphs into one of horror and raw grief, and I smile, if a little sadly. "You were right all along."

I dart away from the grave without warning, and the dog barks, lunges, bone-crushing jaws snapping at my legs. I can already feel the pain that will come when it tears into my flesh, and I squeeze my eyes shut, bracing. But Nimbus, dear Nimbus, leaps from her hiding place among the oak branches and lands on his head, biting, scratching, and clawing, giving me time to get away.

I take it, hike up my skirts, and run down the drive, out the gate, and across the moor. I can hear D'arcy and Cairn chasing me. The heavy pounding of their boots. Their rapid breathing. How they shout for me to stop, to come back. Only I don't stop, and they don't catch me. I am too swift, my feet sure of every place to step, avoiding the boggy places, my legs strong and hardy.

When I reach the cliffs, I skid to a stop. Gravel bites into the bare skin of my heels, and more cascades over the edge, tumbling down the rock face toward the water below. I lean forward, watching its progress until it lands with tiny splashes in the seafoam, then is immediately covered by a crashing wave.

"Clare!"

D'arcy has reached me, Cairn not far behind, and I

spin to face out to ward him off.

"Stay back, D'arcy! Don't come any closer."

"Clare, enough."

He ignores me, taking another step toward me, and I take one back. The edge of the cliff crumbles slightly under my weight. Now he stops, looking at me fearfully. Though whether he is afraid of me or of losing me, I do not know. Maybe both.

"Whoa. Easy. It's only me. I'm not going to hurt you. Come away from there before you fall, all right?"

I shake my head, laughing as desperation bubbles in my chest. "And if I do? Then what? You'll take me back to the house? Arrest me? Lock me away in an asylum?"

"Clare, please." His voice is low, beseeching. "You need help. Whatever Lir did, whatever happened between the two of you, I only want to help. Please. Let me help you." He holds out his hand.

I look over my shoulder at the ocean, the birthplace of the first nature witch. It is so beautiful and blue, seeming to stretch forever beyond the horizon, that what little bit of my heart is still whole breaks at the sight. "I'm sorry. I can't." I turn back to look at him. "If I do, you'll take me away from him, and I can't be separated from him." I shift my gaze to Cairn and stare into his eyes one last time. "I won't be."

My husband doesn't see it coming. Yet D'arcy must know what I am about to do because he reaches for me as I tip back, arms outstretched. He is too slow, and I fall, my feet leaving the cliff and wind tearing at my hair and clothes.

For a moment, I think I see Lir looking down at me from the sky. On either of him stand two women, one dressed all in white, with golden hair and bright blue eyes, the other in dark robes, her face half hidden behind her wild

207

mane of red hair, a crow on her shoulder.

Brigid and the Morrigan.

They have come to take me home, to be with my love forever, and I close my eyes, smiling as my body hits the water, welcoming the pain that is followed almost instantly by darkness.

I am free at last.

Acknowledgments

This book was originally meant to be a retelling of the life and times of Edgar Allan Poe. Along with being a huge fan of his work, I have always been oddly fascinated with the mystery surrounding Poe's death, and having just read The Raven's Tale by Cat Winters—which is by far the best-written, most historically accurate Poe retelling ever, in my opinion—I was inspired to try my hand at writing a historical fiction murder mystery cross over that would take place after he died.

Looking back, I can almost hear Clare laughing at me from the shadows of my mind as I typed and then threw away terrible draft after terrible draft. It wasn't until two years after I gave up on the manuscript and put the project back on the shelf to collect dust for good that she finally decided I was ready to tell her story and emerged in full color. I was listening to an herbalism episode of the Witch Wave podcast at the time, and when they started talking about sage, she jumped out at me and yelled, "Hey! That's me!" I nearly drove my car off the road, she scared me so badly lol.

I will be forever grateful that, of all the storytellers she could have chosen to pen her macabre heart-beneath-the-floorboards (or, in this case, garden) tale, she found me worthy.

I get asked a lot how writing a story works. My answer is always the same: that the stories which hold the most power for me are the ones where my characters communicate with me. They tell me their story, the words flowing from them to me like water, and I pour it out onto paper.

I have heard many different theories about these

"voices in writer's heads." That they are spirits from another time whose memories linger in the ether, waiting to be pulled out again by those who can hear them. Entities from another realm who speak to us through visions. The result of active imagination, or something else entirely. I think they are the secrets that live inside every one of us, born of experiences and kept locked away in hidden places until we are ready to set them free. A proverbial Pandora's Box. And to me, this makes these characters, in a way, as real as you and me, yet at the same time, something completely magical and other.

So, while this story still is, at its heart—no pun intended—a Poe retelling of The Tell-Tale Heart with elements of The Raven, The Golden Bug, The Masque of the Red Death, The Cask of Amontillad, and, yes, a poet who meets an untimely end, it is also a story about outcast women, our society's prejudice toward them, and the dangerous affect that abandonment can have on their mental health, told from one very broken, very angry girl's perspective. As someone who not only loves EAP but has dealt with mental health issues since my teen years, that makes it near and dear to my heart in a way which no other book I've written can claim.

Thanks to God, Who has carved out every path, every experience, that has led me where I am today. Who gifted me the talent to seek out and find these secret tales and weave them into something whole and literary.

To Dani, for loving this story as much as I did and helping me grow it from a plain little seed into something truly dark and beautiful.

To my Insta writing crew – Jordan, Dallas, Brandy, B. K., Nicole, Liz, Ashley, Audra, C. V., Dawn, Sarah, Amber, Lindsey, De, Kalie, Madison, Holly, Faith, Ashley, Nicole (yes, there's two of them), Kacey, K. C. – thank you for the solidarity in being afraid of our own spooky stories while running through the house turning all the lights on to banish the shadows and refusing to sleep alone, sharing in the mutual weirdness that is having multiple voices in your head trying to tell you their tales, gushing over one another's covers like they're the Lost Ark of the Covenant, never getting tired of reading and blurbing early copies of each other's works, the fluffy bunny memes that made me smile when my edits made me want to pull out my hair, and so many book recs our TBRs will never recover. Publishing can be a dark and scary place sometimes, and knowing that I have such a magical group of story sisters in my corner is something I will never stop being grateful for.

To Shannon and the incredible team at R&R Book Tours for another great ARC tour and cover reveal. I honestly don't know how I would get the word out about my books to readers without you.

To Faye, for once again reaching into your hat and creating the most beautiful, magical cover I could ever have imagined for this book.

To my family, who remain my biggest supporters and first viewers. If I didn't have you all in my corner to read rough drafts that I would never let anyone else see and oh and ah over cover art and title ideas, I do not know what I would do. But it's probably somewhere along the idea of hiding under a blanket all day, afraid to show my work to the world.

To Rayne—no matter how good I get at this writing thing, there will never be words to describe how much you mean to me. I know I'm not allowed to call you princess anymore, because to you that means frilly pink dresses and tiaras atop curly hair and long, lame days spent waiting in a tower for a handsome prince to rescue you when you could be playing softball outside instead. But to me, a princess is what you will always be, because of the kindness and beauty you embody, inside and out. You are the strength I work out in order to have, the independence I lost then found again. Your confidence shines brighter than any crown ever could, and you wear ripped jeans and a t-shirt with the same kind of self-imposed grace as Cinderella did with a gown and glass slippers. I pray every day that you always remember who you are. That you never lose sight of what's important in life, and that God never stops guiding you on your journey to the throne. Know that you are the reason I write, that you are the magic that inspires my every word. I love you more than words, more than life, more than breath.

And to everyone who is reading this book right now—thank you from the bottom of my twisted, beating heart. It means more than I can say that you picked up my dark little book and traveled through the pages to the oak tree with me. I hope the light on the other side isn't too bright for you.

Praise for Song of the Cicadas

"Raw, mysterious, and beautiful. The perfect story to keep you engaged until the end. Holt weaves a magical story you will not want to put down." - Brandy Nacole, International Bestselling Author of *Deep in the Hollow*, *The Shadow World Trilogy*, and *Murder is a Debate*

"Wow, this story! Laura Holt's writing has such a way that is rich, vivid, and lyrical, immersing you deeper and deeper into her characters' world. Gripping from beginning to end. A healthy mix of suspense, supernatural, romance and mystery." - Ashley Slaughter, Award Winning Author of *Of Deceit and Snow* and *Of Legends and Roses*

About the Author

Laura Holt is the award-winning author of the YA Star-Crossed series and Village of Salt and Sorrow. Her poetry, nonfiction, and short fiction have been published in Calla Press, Pegasus Literary Magazine, Ginosko Literary Journal, Folkways Press Right to Life Anthology, Clever Fox Literary, and the Eber & Wein 2015 Anthology. She is a self-professed word witch with a passion for mythology, history, and caffeine who enjoys telling stories about angry girls with magic powers and wild natures, whose bark is as bad as their bite. When she's not writing, you can find her stretched out on a yoga mat, hiking down wooded trails, or wandering the aisles at a local bookstore searching for her next great read. She lives in small-town Georgia with her daughter, three cats, and a lot of fake plants.

Follow her on Instagram @authorlauraholt to stay up to date on bookish news, events, and book and music recs, or subscribe to her monthly newsletter for even more exclusive content and writer resources at https://holtlara2.wixsite.com/lauraholt.

Milton Keynes UK
Ingram Content Group UK Ltd.
UKHW010643290424
441924UK00006B/509